Praise for Daniel Woodrell's

THE MAID'S VERSION

Named a Best Book of the Year
Slate, Washington Post, NPR, *Wall Street Journal,*
Kansas City Star, St. *Louis Post-Dispatch*

"In fewer than 200 pages, but with a richness of theme
and character worthy of the weightiest Victorian novel,
Woodrell brings West Table to life in the varied experiences of its sons and daughters. Woodrell's economical
prose echoes with the flinty cadences of rural speech
and the poetry of the Bible.... *The Maid's Version* affirms
Daniel Woodrell's unique niche in American literature."
— Wendy Smith, *Washington Post*

"Exquisite.... Woodrell orchestrates a captivating, almost
operatic narrative of how tragedy and grief can transform
places and people.... With an economical brilliance similar to that of Denis Johnson in *Train Dreams,* Woodrell
delivers a stunning story of one small town, and all of its
profound complexities and opaque mysteries. It's a considerable achievement, and a pleasure to read."
— S. Kirk Walsh, *New York Times Book Review*

"I'd gladly sign a petition to see Mr. Woodrell included on
any roll call of America's finest living writers."
— Sam Sacks, *Wall Street Journal*

"Further proof, as if we needed it, that Daniel Woodrell is a writer to cherish." —Adam Woog, *Seattle Times*

"In the end, no clear answer to the mystery emerges, but we don't need one. In the morally complex universe of *The Maid's Version,* forgiveness and redemption lie not in punishing the guilty but in bringing all the facts to light, thereby restoring the humanity of a community once devastated by losses greater than it could bear." —Gina Webb, *Atlanta Journal-Constitution*

"It's a whodunit of sorts, but most of all *The Maid's Version* is a portrait of the intricate ways class affects life in seemingly simple, small-town America.... A distinctive blend of lush metaphor and brisk storytelling." —Laura Miller, *Salon*

"*The Maid's Version* is a superbly textured novel....Readers will be reminded once again why critics so often compare Woodrell to William Faulkner and Cormac McCarthy." —Bruce DeSilva, Associated Press

"For readers new to Daniel Woodrell's work, *The Maid's Version* is a perfect introduction and an invitation to read more. It's a short book...but there are lifetimes captured here." —Ellah Allfrey, NPR's *All Things Considered*

"Flawless." —Lisa Shea, *Elle*

"*The Maid's Version* is a whodunit, but really it's the who and not the dun that stays with you: Characters are drawn with such skill and sympathy that every fate resonates." —Leah Greenblatt, *Entertainment Weekly*

"What Woodrell shares with Denis Johnson isn't what most critics believe—the poetical assertion of derelict male initiative—but rather a genius for compression. The much-lauded Woodrellian prose continues to dazzle with its demotic/poetic cadences. . . . It's simple to see in Whitman or Hopkins how style cannot be disjoined from substance, but we forget that the same holds for the most potent prose writers. . . . Despite being emphatically rooted in the dirt and blood of daily living, Woodrell's world is pitched forever towards mythos. . . . For all his emphasis on the origins and repercussions of pain in individual lives, Woodrell is, like every truly great novelist, a mythmaker with both eyes on the absolute. . . . From the start Woodrell has been demonstrating that his true subject is neither the articulation of Ozark masculinity nor the necessity of violence, but loyalty. . . . *The Maid's Version* is one more resplendent trophy on the shelf of an American master." —William Giraldi, *Daily Beast*

"*The Maid's Version* delivers a deeply observed, earthily resonant, and finely sculptured work of American fiction. . . . Reverberating language worthy of that other Missourian, Mark Twain." —Steve Paul, *Kansas City Star*

"*The Maid's Version* will sweep readers away.... Woodrell knows how to command a reader's attention—not so much with plot twists, but with well-built sentences. They can sound almost biblical, if the Bible had been written in the Ozarks."   —Bob Minzesheimer, *USA Today*

"Daniel Woodrell is the American writer we increasingly look to for the latest urgent news on the American soul. *The Maid's Version* is a beautiful engine of a novel, whose cogs were not entirely made by human agency, one might hazard to say. As regards the level of reading pleasure, the highest. As regards the level of literary achievement, the highest."   —Sebastian Barry, author of *On Canaan's Side*

"Less a mystery than a meditation on the mystery of loss.... Long regarded as a regional writer, Woodrell is finally coming to be regarded as merely an excellent one, region notwithstanding. The historical novel is ambitious new terrain for him."   —Alexander Nazaryan, *Atlantic Wire*

"Gorgeously gritty.... Inspired by true events, Daniel Woodrell's probing, powerful tenth work of fiction confirms his status as one of our finest little-known writers."
          —Leigh Haber, *O, The Oprah Magazine*

"Woodrell captures the run-down, put-upon underbelly of America better than anyone.... His die-hard fans range from celeb chef Anthony Bourdain to bestselling authors Annie Proulx and Dennis Lehane."—Benjamin Percy, Esquire.com

"Using a Faulknerian shifting-perspective narrative, Woodrell takes readers through the tangled lives of the victims toward a central story of attraction and betrayal."

—Joe Fassler, *The Atlantic*

"Daniel Woodrell is a genius of bad mojo and a master craftsman of astonishment. *The Maid's Version* is a stunning addition to his growing body of singular American novels. It will twist you and turn you, but mostly it will haunt you."

—Luis Alberto Urrea,
author of *The Hummingbird's Daughter*

"*The Maid's Version* is stunning. Daniel Woodrell writes flowing, cataclysmic prose with the irresistible aura of fate about it."

—Sam Shepard

"Told in meandering flashbacks with a lyrical cadence, the story is gripping and heartrending at the same time.... With *The Maid's Version,* Woodrell confirms his place among the literary masters."

—Elizabeth Dickie, *Booklist*

"No craftsman toiling away in a workshop ever fashioned his wares so carefully. A commanding fable about trespass and reconstruction from a titan of southern fiction."

—*Kirkus Reviews*

"The economy of Woodrell's prose, along with startling turns of phrase that seem like pure poetry, has made him a writer's writer."

—David S. Cohen, *Variety*

"The clans, strivers, adulterers, and outlaws familiar to Woodrell's readers are still around, but his focus has shifted from their estrangement to their convergence. These are townsfolk—not quite blood relations, but nonetheless bound."   —Dwyer Murphy, *Guernica*

"Woodrell's evocative, lyrical ninth novel is deceptively brief and packs a shimmering, resonant, literary punch.... From an economy of poetic prose springs forth an emotionally volcanic story of family, justice, and the everlasting power of the truth."   —*Publishers Weekly*

"Woodrell's lush yet restrained prose beautifully limns the indignities and inequalities that make small-town life into a powder keg waiting for a spark.... Rambling along with the unrushed rhythm of the porch swing, Woodrell's prose begs to be read aloud." —Amy Gentry, *Chicago Tribune Printers Row*

"*The Maid's Version* is spooky and bold, like all Woodrell's work, to the point and out into the darkness."
                        —Jeff Baker, *The Oregonian*

"Woodrell's distinctive qualities are his very puckish humor and the way he drapes extravagantly writerly prose on the bones of a ferociously exciting whodunit.... Writerly writing is easily overpraised. Woodrell's earns its keep."
                        —Sam Leith, *Literary Review*

"Daniel Woodrell has made a name as a master of prose with personality—a densely descriptive, gamey form of storytelling.... *The Maid's Version* is an exploration of the psychology of trauma, the roles and labels given to individuals in societies, as well as the relationship of poverty to impotence, of wealth to immunity, of sex to power."

—Sarah Hall, *The Guardian* (UK)

"*The Maid's Version* is richly peopled, intensely human, irresistibly readable.... Much more than a mystery story, as Woodrell, through a grandmother's tales, burrows into the maelstrom of life in a small town in America."

—Harper Barnes, *St. Louis Post-Dispatch*

THE MAID'S VERSION

A Novel

Daniel Woodrell

BACK BAY BOOKS

LITTLE, BROWN AND COMPANY

New York   Boston   London

Back Bay Books / Little, Brown and Company
Hachette Book Group
237 Park Avenue, New York, NY 10017
littlebrown.com

Originally published in hardcover by Little, Brown and Company, September 2013
First Back Bay trade paperback edition, September 2014

Back Bay Books is an imprint of Little, Brown and Company. The Back Bay Books name and logo are trademarks of Hachette Book Group, Inc.

The publisher is not responsible for websites (or their content) that are not owned by the publisher.

The Hachette Speakers Bureau provides a wide range of authors for speaking events. To find out more, go to hachettespeakersbureau.com or call (866) 376-6591.

Excerpt from "Timber" by Rolf Jacobsen from *North in the World: Selected Poems of Rolf Jacobsen,* translated by Roger Greenwald. English translations © 1985, 1997, 2002 by Roger Greenwald. All rights reserved. Reprinted with permission from the University of Chicago Press.

Library of Congress Control Number 2013937480
ISBN 978-0-316-20585-6 (hc) / 978-0-316-20588-7 (pb)

10 9 8 7 6 5 4 3 2 1

RRD–C

Printed in the United States of America

In memory of Grif Fariello

These are the things the starry sky is set above:
loneliness of the dead, courage of youth, and timber
that's carried slowly away on great rivers.
                                                    —*Rolf Jacobsen*

A wounded deer leaps highest.

—*Emily Dickinson*

Thou desirest truth in the inward parts.

—*Psalms 51:6*

THE MAID'S VERSION

She frightened me at every dawn the summer I stayed with her. She'd sit on the edge of her bed, long hair down, down to the floor and shaking as she brushed and brushed, shadows ebbing from the room and early light flowing in through both windows. Her hair was as long as her story and she couldn't walk when her hair was not woven into dense braids and pinned around and atop her head. Otherwise her hair dragged the floor like the train of a medieval gown and she had to gather it into a sheaf and coil it about her forearm several times to walk the floor without stepping on herself. She'd been born a farm girl, then served as a maid for half a century, so she couldn't sleep past dawn to win a bet, and all the mornings I knew with her she'd sit in the first light and brush that witchy-long hair, brush it in sections, over and over, stroking hair that had scarcely been touched by scissors for decades, hair she would not part with despite the extravagance of time it required at each dawn. The hair was mostly white smeared by gray, the hues of a newspaper that lay in the rain until headlines blended across the page.

She spooked me awake daily that whole summer of my twelfth year, me awaking to see her with the dawn at her back, springs squeaking faintly, while a bone-handled brush slid along a length of hair that belonged in a fairy tale of some sort, and maybe not the happy kind. Her name was Alma and she did not care to be called Grandma or Mamaw, and might loose a slap if addressed as Granny. She was lonely, old and proud, and I'd been sent from my river town near St. Louis by my dad as a gesture of reconciliation. She was glad I'd been sent and concerned that I have a good time, a memorable summer, but she was not naturally given to much frolic; the last hours of play she'd known had been before World War I, some game now vanished from childhood that involved a rolling wooden hoop and a short stick. She tried taking me for long walks about the town of West Table, going to People's Park so she could watch me splash in the pool, let me pull weeds in the garden and throw a baseball against the toolshed door. It was the summer of 1965, but she still did not have a television, only a radio that seemed always to be announcing livestock prices and yield estimates. There was a twang stretching every word Alma said, but for days and days she didn't say much. Then came a late afternoon when I was dramatically dispirited, moody and bored, foot idly kicking at things I'd been told not to kick, a sweltering day that turned dark as a sinister storm settled overhead, and we sat together on her small porch in a strong wind to watch those vivid actions break across the sky. Storm clouds were scored by bright lightning, and thunder boomed. Her dress was flapping, her eyes narrowed and distant, and she cunningly chose that raging moment to begin telling me her personal account of the Arbor Dance Hall explosion of 1929, how forty-two dancers from this small corner of the Missouri Ozarks had perished in an instant, waltzing couples murdered midstep, blown toward the clouds in a pink mist chased by towering flames, and why it happened. This was more like it— an excitement of fire, so many fallen, so many suspects, so few facts, a great crime or colossal accident, an ongoing mystery she thought she'd solved. I knew this was a story my dad did not want me to hear from her lips, as it was a main source of their feud, so I was tickled and keen to hear more, more, and then more. Dozens were left maimed, broken in their parts, scorched until skin melted from bones. The screams from the rubble and flames never faded from the ears of those who heard them, the cries of burning neighbors, friends, lovers, and kinfolk like my great-aunt Ruby. So many young dead or ruined from a town of only four thousand raised a shocked, grievous howling for justice. Suspicions were given voice, threats shouted, mobs gathered, but there was no obvious target for all the summoned fury. Suspects and possible explanations for the blast were so numerous and diverse, unlinked by convincing evidence, that the public investigation spun feebly in a wide, sputtering circle, then was quietly closed. No one was ever officially charged nor punished, and the twenty-eight unidentified dead were buried together beneath a monumental angel that stood ten feet tall and slowly turned black during year after year of cold and hot and slapping rain.

Alma yet lived in a small room with a small kitchen in the back portion of her last employer's house, and it was tight living. Her bed and the couch I slept on were five feet apart. Her sleep was chatty; she had one-way chats with people she'd once known or her sleep invented. She sometimes mumbled names I'd heard around the dinner table. She often wept without sound at night until tears shined her neck, and made dull daytime company for a boy unless she was adding wrinkles to her story. When in the telling mood she'd sit on the porch for hours staring toward the dry white creek bed out back while drinking tea to keep her voice slickened, leaving each used tea bag in the cup when adding a fresh one and more water, soaking every penny's worth of tea into her cup until she sipped bitter trickles between four or five derelict bags. She would at times leave the public horror and give me her quiet account of the sad and criminal love affair that took her sister Ruby away from us all, left us with only pain, many dark mysteries, and a woman's hat with a long feather in the band.

Alma had been allowed to stay in school to the completion of third grade, then was sent to work some years in her daddy's fields before finding her way to town and becoming a laundress, a cook, an all-purpose maid. She lost two sons along the way, her husband, her sister, and earned but little, always one dropped dish and a loud reprimand from complete and utter poverty. She lived scared and angry, a life full of permanent grievances, sharp animosities and cold memories for all who'd ever crossed us, any of us, ever. Alma DeGeer Dunahew, with her pinched, hostile nature, her dark obsessions and primal need for revenge, was the big red heart of our family, the true heart, the one we keep secret and that sustains us.

It was years before I learned to love her.

Our long walks that summer did if nothing else prepare me to accept an early bedtime, for they were tiring and detailed. At any corner or alleyway, empty lot or spruced old house, she was liable to stop and leave me in her mind, revisiting yet again insults she couldn't forgive. "That place there was home to Mrs. Prater, who cheated me of near eleven dollars when your uncle Sidney was a-dyin' in bed with no medicine for the pain. He moaned constant as the wind and couldn't catch his breath. Not even fourteen years old. She had her a few daughters, and one has married here and stayed—her children are named Cozzens. Couple of boys. Your big brother could whup either of them pukes this minute without even needin' to put his sandwich down. Years to come you'll thrash 'em, too, if you should be so blessed as to come across one somewhere behind a building, or in the trees, and hear that name."

Or she'd drift in thought while staring at an empty spread of dirt and grass between two homes, and say,

"Used to be a house here had a porch that went all the way around, with strangler vines growing up the sides, had those windows like eyes up top. Mr. Lee Haas lived there. He run the last dry goods near the square that would give us anything on tick. But his wife squawked over me bein' crazy and full of slander, the fool, and he cut me dead when most needed. That year was 1933, I think." She waved a big old withering hand at the lot where the house had been, spit toward the grass but fell short, so she stepped fully into the lot and spit again. "But you can forget them—God done for them, and done 'em up good, too, during the war."

On these rambles the cemetery was nearly always our final destination. We'd make our way through the wilderness of headstones, gray, brown, puritan white, glancing at some, nodding at some, Alma turning her nose up at others, until we reached the Black Angel, the sober monument to our family loss and a town bereaved. Standing in the shadow of this angel she would on occasion tell me about a suspect person or deed, a vague or promising suspicion she'd acquired with her own sharp ears or general snooping, and when she shared the fishy details with me it would be the first time she'd said them aloud to anybody in years. She'd repeat herself so I'd remember. We'd then walk home, going into the fat shade under the fat trees on East Main, and stop at Jupiter Grocery, where she always said, "Your momma's grandpa on her momma's side worked here thirty years. He cut a good piece of meat."

We'd prowl the aisles and assemble the evening meal, a meal usually made of the cheapest foodstuffs, some of which I'd never before considered as food and was scared to touch—calves' brains to be served with scrambled eggs, souse for sandwiches I'd throw behind the shed, pigs' feet and saltines, pork rind and corn pone, chicken livers by the pound that she rendered into a bizarre gravy that was so surprisingly fine over egg noodles or white rice that I learned to whine for it as we walked. We'd eat together in her snug quarters, an early supper, always, elbow to elbow, watching squares of sunlight lose their shape along the walls, and return to the unending topic while forks clicked on her best plates, "What'd you learn today, Alek, and what use will you make of it?"

And Alma did that summer make certain that I knew this spot and that these pictures would be planted in my head, grow epic, never leave: The Arbor Dance Hall stood across the street from a row of small houses and one still stands. A house with nothing to recommend it but its age, shown up meanly in sunlight and made to look ancient in shadow. The yard between the house and the railroad tracks has become a worn patch of dust, the old oaks have withered from their long days and begun to founder toward earth, and no new neighbors have been built. In 1929, on this narrow span of sloping ground between the town square and the tracks beside Howl Creek, there had been six houses, five now gone, the dance hall, and the long-demolished Alhambra Hotel. At the bottom of the yard near the railroad ties and shined rails there are burnished little stumps where elms that likely witnessed everything had been culled in the 1950s after the Dutch blight moved into town and caught them all.

The explosion happened within a shout and surely those in the house must have heard everything on that bright evening, the couples arriving, strolling arm in arm or as foursomes, the excited laughter, the cooed words, the stolen kisses on the way to the dance, all carrying loudly on that blossom-scented night between the wars, here in the town this was then of lulled hearts and distracted spirits. A Saturday of sunshine, the town square bunched with folks in for trading from the hills and hollers, hauling spinach, lettuce and rhubarb, chickens, goats and alfalfa honey. Saturday crowds closed the streets around the square and it became a huge veranda of massed amblers. Long hellos and nodded goodbyes. Farmers in bib overalls with dirty seats, sporting dusted and crestfallen hats, raising pocket hankies already made stiff and angular with salt dried from sweat during the slow wagon ride to town. In the shops and shade there are others, wearing creased town clothes, with the immaculate hankies of gentlefolk folded to peak above breast pockets in a perfect suggestion of gentility and standing. The citizenry mingled—Howdy, Hello, Good gracious is that you? The hardware store is busy all day and the bench seats outside become heavy with squatting men who spit brown splotches toward the gutter. Boys and girls hefted baskets of produce, munched penny candy, and begged nickels so they could catch the matinee at the Avenue Theater. Automobiles and trucks park east of the square, wagons and mules rest north in the field below the stockyard pens, and after supper folks made their way downhill to the Arbor...and just as full darkness fell those happy sounds heard in the surviving house suddenly became a nightmare chorus of pleas, cries of terror, screams as the flames neared crackling and bricks returned tumbling from the heavens and stout beams crushed those souls knocked to ground. Walls shook and shuddered for a mile around and the boom was heard faintly in the next county south and painfully by everyone inside the town limits. Citizens came out their doors, stunned, alarmed to stillness, then began to sprint, trot, stagger in flailing and confused strides toward this new jumping light that ate into the night.

A near portion of the sky founted an orange brilliance in a risen tower, heat bellowing as flames freshened in the breeze and grew, the tower of orange tilting, tossing about, and the sounds dancers let loose began to reach distant ears as anonymous wails and torture those nearby with their clarity of expression. There were those who claimed to have heard words of farewell offered by victims in the air or in the rubble, and some must be true accounts; so many citizens crawled into the flames to pull at blistered, smoking bodies that turned out to be people they knew, sisters, uncles, sons or pals. As with any catastrophe, the witness accounts immediately began to differ, as some saw dancers blown three hundred feet toward the stars and spreading in a spatter of directions, while others saw them go no more than a hundred and fifty feet high, give or take, though all agreed that several fortunate souls were saved from death by the force of their throwing, landing beyond reach of the scorching, pelted with falling debris, yes, and damaged, but not roasted skinless, hairless, blackened and twisted on their bones.

The nearest witness to survive and offer prompt testimony was eighty-nine-year-old Chapman Eades, an ex-Confederate, veteran of Pea Ridge and the siege of Vicksburg, who lived in the Alhambra. He did not see well and could not follow a conversation in his own little room without the aid of an ear trumpet. The next day Mr. Eades said to the West Table *Scroll,* "I don't know what they was arguin' about. They was over behind the back wall and I never seen them as nothin' but shapes standin' in shadows. But they was arguin' about somethin' awful lively, then the music struck up again and all hell came callin' soon after."

Throughout that summer human scraps and remains were discovered in gardens two streets, three streets, four streets away, kicked up in the creek by kids chasing crawdads, in deep muck at the stockyards halfway up the hill. That fall, when roof gutters were cleaned, so many horrid bits were come across that gutters became fearsome, hallowed, and homeowners let a few respectful leaks develop that winter rather than disturb the dead.

My mother was never poor until she married. She was born a Hudkins, her place in the world was not Alma's, and she'd first met my father when he was the paper boy and she swooned for his dimples and blue eyes. She would've been around eight or ten (depending on what her true birth date is, for several have been claimed) and he was fourteen or so. The house had been given a name, even, called Hudkins, a large and comfortable old home with a full city block for a backyard, all fenced with white rails, two horses grazing or snuffling from the trough, a serviceable pickup truck parked in the dirt drive, a new sedan in the garage, the gray walls of the cemetery ever visible just beyond the farthest rails and across one street. Mother pestered Dad with friendly comments and he suspected mockery, mockery of everything about him, from boondockers held together with twine to his bib overalls that fit him better a year earlier and his sullied name, so he stooped to ground and raised to throw rocks at her without trying to bruise or come too close. She never forgot the excitement of having his full attention. Years later, while Dad was home on leave during the final hours of World War II, they locked eyes at the Echo Club, she in a pink sweater and saddle shoes, he wearing his navy hat cocked saltily, the band playing swing, and both remembered the rocks. Nature did the rest and they married soon. Her father, Harlan Hudkins, never forgave Dad for knocking her up so young (Mom would lose the first two babies and feel doomed until a robust boy survived to be born in 1950), or her for being weak to a goddam Dunahew, no matter how sweetly he danced, and he had his ways of making everybody pay, even his only blue-eyed grandson, though I was always told to feel welcome, just come on by, and did visit happily many, many times. He was a big rugged man with a fabled past in athletics, wearing a Stetson hat colored pearl, a Roi-Tan cigar chomped between his teeth, owner of a feed mill, a few rental properties and several tracts of timberland. Harlan hunted often, for quail locally and pheasant up north, and kept bird dogs, three or four at a time, penned out behind the house. After the marriage of my parents he named every dog he had, or would ever have, Buster, the nickname of Alma's husband. Both of my brothers could step into a Hudkins family photo from any era and blend—I am all Dunahew in appearance, and Harlan noticed. I had a choked, complicated regard for him, he was a powerful presence with so many qualities boys admire, but I identified as a Dunahew in my bones and attitudes, grandson of a drunken bum and a maid who couldn't read a grocery list, and said so often. Harlan heard me.

The Black Angel standing over the unidentified dead started to dance in 1989. Folks laying wreaths saw the angel shimmy her hips just a little and called for more witnesses and there were indeed more small attempts at divine dancing observed, so the newspaper was notified. The tombstone the angel stood atop was as long as two men, crowded with names chiseled into marble decades ago, but still shiny. The Black Angel towered and held a torch overhead, in case, I suppose, Truth tried to sneak past in the dark. The flame had also turned black.

My dad was in town, visiting Harlan, now all alone in a big house, and I helped the old man to the cemetery where everybody he ever loved but one are buried. His heart was shot, he walked on flimsy legs with short careful steps, and I carried his cigarettes, flask of Cutty Sark and a folding chair for him to rest on. An article in the *Scroll* attracted a pack of goth and stoner gawkers, spiritualists and ghost hunters, relatives of those below, and a lady reporter from the biggest Springfield television station. This assembly spent two evenings there, next to the monument, with big lights lit, reading over and again the names of the dead dancers spread chiseled into three columns. The names were yet known to many (great disasters being so diligently committed to memory and passed on) and kin to a few of us gathered there, the pious or merely hopeful holding candles and runt crosses while the scientific fiddled with special cameras and infrared doodads.

During the first night the congregated dead below had been made bashful by so much strange company and not stirred a bit. Those present remained good-humored and interested, learning the repeated names (Powell, Mulvein, Breen, Gutermuth, Campbell, Steinkuhler, McCandless, Shelton, Shelton, Shelton, Gower, Bullington, Bullington, Boardman, DeGeer...) until the roll call became a chant sung by a diverse crowd, then disbanded shortly after midnight.

Dad had a great time with the crowd and told as many stories as he heard.

At the second vigil the litany of names began again at dark and soon acquired a lulling meter, a pacifying drone that was maintained for two hours, until we all suddenly saw the same thing and popped to our feet. The crowd gasped in unison like a practiced choir. The Black Angel jigged an inch left, jigged an inch right, then ever so slightly to and fro. There was a general rush toward the hem of her skirt. I walked to the monument and rested my head against it, fingers tangled across all those names, palm flattened flush against Ruby's. They'd been down there so long—why dance now? They surely did feel to be dancing, though, the angel trembling above as those souls below did the Lindy Hop, an aggrieved variation of it, I would suppose, but their young rhythm and spring could be felt through the stone and decades.

Dad shoved up from his chair, limped to my side, laid his hand over mine.

The spiritualists and goths beamed haughtily as though publicly vindicated, the stoners cackled until told to hush, the gathered relatives seemed to slump in recognition of an old responsibility to their own lost kin that they had long ago put aside when frazzled apathetic by too many mysteries and myriad angles, but might now need to resurrect. The scientific debunkers held forth about karst topography and caves riddling our hillsides but the big lights were extinguished even as they spoke.

As the crowd departed and we wended through the ranks of dead, then began crossing the street to Hudkins, Dad rested a hand on my shoulder, squeezed as strongly as he could but weakly, then said, "Tell it. Go on and tell it."

She hated that she fed another man's children before she fed her own. She cleared the supper table, the plates yet rife with food in this house of plenty, potatoes played with, bread crusts stacked on the tablecloth unwanted, meat bones set aside with enough shreds on them to set her own sons fighting one another for a chance to gnaw them clean and white. Her own sons sucked cold spuds at home, waiting. The Glencross kids, Ethan and Virginia, both handsome and bossy for their years, dawdled over their suppers with great disinterest until released from the table by their father. In the kitchen Alma took the bones and rolled them inside a page of newspaper, tucked the paper under her dress and into the thieving belt she wore hidden. Her own sons waited. She used the blade of her hands to shove the leavings from the plates into the slop bucket and carried the slop out back, across the big grand yard to the wire dog pen, bent and poured it into the rusted bowl as lonely Kaiser Bill licked her hands.

The kitchen had been cleaned, made orderly and plain, and she was about to sling the wet rag over the faucet to dry and be off and away, when Ethan and Virginia clomped into the kitchen and told her they were famished, suddenly terribly famished, and would Alma oblige them each with another plate of supper, and heat the cowboy gravy again, please. Alma set out plates she'd just washed and dried, scraped at with fingernails while dunking her hands into chilling water, then opened the icebox and felt about for bowls of leftovers. Her own sons waited at home, stomachs pinging, hoping tonight there'd be food that had a bone in it, or at least food that had once lived on a bone. A flame sparked, the pots went on the blue rings of fire, and as she stirred with a wooden spoon the kids wandered into the parlor, then she heard them climbing the stairs, going to their rooms, doors clicking shut.

She waited while the gravy cooled again.

She cleaned the pots once more, put everything away, and as she walked toward the door, Mr. Arthur Glencross, president of Citizens' Bank, a guarded but approachable man whose many good qualities were well known and celebrated while his lesser qualities were excused, beckoned Alma near, and whispered, "She wants me home tonight."

Alma nodded, and went out through the side door, across the lawn to the alleyway in back. The alley was unlighted but offered the quickest route toward home, and she was guided over the slumping dirt and scattered stones by brightness from neighboring windows and the memory in her feet. The alley led to an avenue. Big trees kept the avenue shrouded, but the sidewalk was wide and mostly level underfoot. A cluster of peach trees grew in the large yard of a large old home near the corner where Alma turned south, and she paused there, took a stand near the trees, waiting to hear a voice. The peaches were young, small and hard but beginning to draw the branches down, and the air smelled fertile. She peered between tree trunks and cocked her head to better hear anything said to her from inside that darkness. And in seconds a voice from the peach cluster asked, "Is he in the house?"

"He is."

"He's left me sittin' out here two hours waitin'."

"He's with his wife."

"That nervy bastard."

"She's keepin' him close tonight."

Ruby DeGeer had been squatted to the ground among the peach trees, and now she rose, dusted her behind with a swatting hand and stepped onto the sidewalk. The sisters linked arms and began walking without comment, all the way to the town square and halfway around, then past the stock pens and down the hill toward the Dunahew shack. The pens were empty this night, but still stunk of livestock, a nearly pleasing stench that lingered over the eastern side of town.

"And here I wore my new hat, too."

"I like it—what'd it run?"

"Won't tell."

"He buy you it?"

"No. Somebody else."

The sisters favored as to posture, but Ruby was ten years younger and petite, with brown eyes that were often described in poetic terms, and a beguiling figure that she did not hide behind poorly fitted clothing or a dowdy fashion sense. Her hair was dark, with red aspects from henna she added, and was sculpted into a fashion that had roots in Egyptian myth, with straight, full bangs barely above the eyes and crisply sheared edges at jaw level. She was vivid in nature, sparky and game, and flirted readily with about any presentable man just to make time fly or snag a fatter tip at the Stockman's Café when she waited tables. She'd run away to New Orleans once for three months and returned eager to give the impression that she'd seen many scandalous practices in this wicked old world, but had not been rubbed wrong by too many of them. She smoked Sweet Caporals on the street and laughed out loud in public, sometimes swore, and Alma was fearful for her when she was not jealous.

Alma said, "Will you sleep with us?"

"I've got Irish taters in my bag."

"Them'll go good with these bones I brung."

Alma was of a height that earned no description save "regular," sturdy in her legs and chest, and her hair was an ordinary who-gives-a-hoot brown, with finger waves above the ears that always collapsed into messy curls as the day went along. Kitchen work required her to keep her hair trimmed short to ensure that long hairs did not grace the meals she served. She dressed in whatever clothing Providence provided her and was grateful for anything that fit.

When the sisters went up the stoop to the Dunahew shack their steps were carefully placed on the bad wood of the narrow, askew porch, but they were heard and the door flung open on all three boys gathered just inside, ages thirteen, ten and five in 1929, with thin necks, soiled young hands, and hope verging on greed in their eyes. Alma pulled the bones from the thieving belt under her dress, held them up and said, "There's gonna be supper."

The shack had been poorly made long ago, built to house itinerant folks who'd tended to apple orchards at the eastern edge of town before a variety of wasting blights came along and the trees died, taking two dozen jobs down with them. The front steps sagged under every footstep, and the roof of the house was compromised by rot and spavined, a roofline that slumped in the middle, with holes beneath the eaves that were often used as entrances to the attic by squirrels, and the sounds of toenails clicking across the ceiling became frequent and routine. Inside there were two parts to the only room, divided by a stick-legged table plus three chairs, so both parts were constantly open to view and no one could ever be out of sight. A floor had been made of roughhewn planks that had been slowly rubbed to a haggard softness by clomping boots, wallowing toddlers in flour sack britches, woolen socks sliding, and the brisk sweeps of a corn-husk broom. A noisy pump with a long handle brought water into the kitchen. The sink was not laid level in the kitchen counter, but hoisted higher to the left and wedged in stiff, the result of repairs done almost correctly by Maurice "Buster" Dunahew, Alma's husband. On most days the house held only four people, as Buster was no longer allowed to sleep there, or even visit much since he was required to arrive sober, and Ruby slept over only now and then, whenever blue clouds massing inside her chest raised a need to rest among family.

Alma washed potatoes for the stew while Ruby wrestled on the floor with the two younger boys, Sidney and John Paul. They loved to hug her and feel her arms around their shoulders in return, squeezing them near to smell her perfume, her lipstick, her smoky breath so exciting as it burst onto their faces. Ruby's style, her looks, her sass and vinegar gave them the urge to fight for more, more of everything they could imagine, against anybody, whenever she was near. James was old enough to have heard stories and insults at school that narrowed his horizon in this town to a pinhole and made him more reserved, sullen on most days, with his taut face and slanted eyes. He had recently become captivated by tales of pirates on the high seas and the lucrative derring-do of regional outlaws, and thus inspired had taken to pinching necessary things from those who had them, and Alma did not ask as many questions as she might have done when medicines somehow came into the house, or canned pineapple, long johns, hunks of ham with savory juices that were memorized by the younger boys and described for weeks.

The bones and shreds of meat flavored the broth, and she'd added onions and Irish taters, a few beans from yesterday, a ramshackle stew, but one that should fill every tummy for a night. Alma turned from the stove and spoke in a whisper, "Supper, boys," and she didn't need to whisper twice.

M iss Dimple Powell was fifteen years old and had never been to a dance. She'd prayed this night of music and boys would come before she wasted away from boredom, and had practiced dancing alone in her room for a full year now, her partner an overstuffed pillow with a dashing manner and a rather racy line of patter. His hair lay flat and glossy, shining like Valentino's, and his hands sometimes roamed her back and she'd have to remind him she was fifteen and in no hurry, sir, but not mad, either. Her sister, July, and brother-in-law, Charles Lathrop, had gently hectored Mr. Powell, who had gotten accustomed to hearing the expectant sliding of waltzing feet from the floor above as he read the evening paper, until he said yes, finally, yes, and on dance night he gave Dimple a silent, rueful and humbled look over his spectacles as he watched her leaving his house so beautiful in a spotless new dress.

East Side: dirt streets spread with oil to hold the dust low, home after home where the rough-lumbered walls have been deserted by paint and wasps haunt the eaves: a tin roof the sun beats on nakedly and sears but rainwater glides from smoothly and is gone in a slap into the dirt, it makes reddish mud in the front yard, side yard, backyard. Sidewalks are of little use, usefulness burst by the foraging roots of nearby trees, the wooden planks softened by age and slanted in two directions or more from the corruption in the middle. The sidewalk staves make excellent weapons when weapons are suddenly needed—he's drunk again, that's my bottle of milk, I just don't want you around here no more, got that? Cats prowl between houses, dogs range about in the alleys, and a welter of children with bare feet play in wan, worn yards, beneath fading trees, playing with the terrible intensity of those who know already how quickly passing are their scant hours for fun.

Alma walked from the east each morning toward an important place, a house of prospering girth, brick walls sturdy as a vault, with a shaded veranda and heavy balustrade of purified white, a trefoil arch in the masonry over the doorway, large windows spanned by glass that rippled and bowed in the antique manner, bringing a winsome disarray to the eye from certain angles, the view of the world outside bent as the glass would have it bent, or stretched, or truncated. Town life was not so much run by the sun anymore but by the time displayed on clock faces, though Alma still answered to the early cock crows, roosters across town greeting dawn loudly but not in unison, somehow sensing daylight's arrival with considerable variance of time, some now, some several minutes later. But she would always be at work early enough to make breakfast for Mr. Glencross, a hearty eater—pork sausage, eggs and cream biscuits—then the children, picky and complaining, usually wanting any cereal she hadn't cooked, or eggs if she'd made cereal, and finally Mrs. Glencross, who asked only for cooled toast with no butter or jam and a steaming mug of English tea.

She often ate while standing near the kitchen sink, staring from the window there, and might address Alma as the table was cleared, "Do you believe it could rain today?"

"It could."

"Believe it will?"

"Not likely. We need it too much."

"My poor roses."

Mrs. Glencross was the real source of wealth in the house. She'd been born into the Jarman family, and the

Jarmans owned just about everything they cared to have—giant swaths of Ozark land, cattle, hogs and rental properties, a lumberyard, the Opera House, and a big piece of Citizens' Bank. Mrs. Corinne Glencross had grown up shielded from a rounded experience of life, considered to be so delicate that she must not know the feel of direct sunlight upon her skin, the rude wind, dishwater on her hands, coarse people, and the common gamut of unpleasant facts. She didn't know how to do anything much, but Alma liked her, liked her strange lilting mind, innocent and flitting about airily from subject to subject, making amusing points along the way but not lingering. She had few demands, or at least didn't think of many she cared to utter. She spent the middle hours of most days reclining on the divan in the parlor with the curtains drawn and a cold cloth over her eyes, waiting stoically for her next appointment with Dr. Thomason. When she felt better, peppy for an hour or two, she'd follow Alma around the house as she worked, watching her do laundry, clean all fourteen rooms, make lye soap some days, iron bedsheets others, and ask her why she did things this way instead of that way, or what would happen if you tried dusting with a sponge, or used a more slender stick to stir the clothes in the washtub.

Alma would be patient, try to tell her why, or else say, "You're lookin' peaked just now, Mrs. Glencross. Wouldn't want you to swoon to the floor and bruise. You got such good skin."

On shopping days Alma would stride toward the square with a canvas tote bag and a small wad of money. She liked the meats from Jupiter Grocery, the produce from Widow McLean's, and bought bread at the Greek's down the avenue. When the Greek's opened, Alma had resisted the place for months but relented, and on her first attempt to shop there she felt the Greek was trying to get an advantage on her in the amount of seven cents. She'd eyed him coldly, coin purse clenched unopened in her hand, then said, "You do me thisaway, mister, and you ain't skinnin' me at all—you're skinnin' Mr. Arthur Glencross. You best ask a friend who that is." In the early gloaming of that evening the Greek called at the Glencross house with a heavy sack of hard candy, two loaves of bread, black olives and a long low nod for Alma. The Greek's bread quickly became so highly regarded by the gentry that all the maids were relieved of bread-making duty, and though their gratitude to the Greek went unspoken, they became forever loyal to the store. The four and sometimes five or six maids who worked near the square tried to meet at the Greek's between dusting time and lunch. They fingered the jars of interesting foods, smelled the coffee beans, and gathered on a bench outside in the shade where they could observe the avenue but were unlikely to be overheard as they sat there telling the truth in whispers or laughing about it with their faces turned to the sky.

R uby DeGeer didn't mind breaking hearts, but she liked them to shatter coolly, with no ugly scenes of departure where an arm got twisted behind her back by a crying man, or her many failings and damp habits were made specific in words shouted out an open window. Accepting boredom did not come easily to her, and some men could bore her beyond courtesy before the first drink was drained or the key rattled into a hotel room door, but if she liked a fella, then he knew unleashed marvels until she didn't anymore and in their fresh agony the heartbroken twisted her arm crying or yelled her business to the street. She'd known poverty from birth but been blessed with pizzazz and understood early that life was a fight and she couldn't win even one round if she kept her best hand tied behind her back. If men were smitten by her lyric eyes and fluctuating mounds and scented sashay, well, let them display their feelings in meaningful ways: clothes, hats, rent, a big weekend at the Peabody in Memphis, a morning visit on Christmas Day when they ought to be home with their wives and children but couldn't stay away, just couldn't do it, just can't.

"Bring me somethin' adorable I want when you come round again."

She'd part from them one by one as the men grew too complicated with their appetites and plans or her dance card became too full with the newly smitten, who tended to splurge more readily anyhow. She'd soon sink the new beneath her blunt desires and work them and work them until the pump handle started to stick, then spring a farewell moment and move along. The money never amounted to all that much, but it now and then bought a few items of worth, some to be worn, some to be polished and saved in a drawer for pawning later, fed her fairly regular meals, helped her rent a private room. It was not prostitution in her view because she did not extract a payment for each intimacy, never did that, never would, but only accepted something more like a sneak tithing from fellas she called friends. "That's just romancin'," she'd say. Wives disagreed and she'd been assaulted a few times, called a dirty-leg whore, bimbo, tramp, had her hair pulled, been kicked blue in the shins, slapped in the face. Alma almost lost her job when she hunted the wife who'd bloodied Ruby's nose on the square and made the lady say "Snuff" with her face pushed against a store window, then suggested in whispers as she pressed from behind that who the lady ought to be hitting was wearing pants and a mustache. (There'd been calls from friends of the whupped lady for Alma to be dismissed, but Mrs. Glencross heard about the encounter, the vulgarity and vigor displayed by women tussling in a public place, the sunlight brilliant on exposed skin, and flushed with secondhand excitement as she listened, then said, "Valiant, so valiant," to describe Alma's defense of Ruby, and that was that.) Such moments were what made sisters special to sisters, and Ruby shared her spoils from the field of *amour* with Alma and the Dunahew boys whenever she had any surplus. Alma did not like the way Ruby lived, had often said so in the sternest tones, but understood too well, too well her baby sister's ravenous need for the comforts and adulation that men provided her, and the savage joy that bounced in her soul whenever she dumped a stricken beau and went out once more dancing alone.

Alma said their early lives had been like this: Cecil DeGeer was white-haired at Alma's birth, and owned with the bank about twenty-five acres across the road from South Turn Creek, maybe fifteen acres in timber and the rest red clay and scrub. They made a huge garden by poaching good soil from the creek bottomland of their neighbor and carrying it away in peach baskets by the light of the moon or in utter darkness. There was no fence line, making it easy to splash buckets from the creek onto row upon row of things to eat if the weather didn't listen to the Devil and blaze or the creek flood again and wash every meal of tomorrow downstream, and run a few hogs in the

brambles and timber. Their mother was a Pruitt with can-
cer of the nose that required a large portion be sliced off,
so she seldom left the land or went among strangers, but
worked long, long, long hours, as though to punish herself
for whatever act or failure cost her that slice of nose. There
was slim reward apparent for her relentless toiling but an
eking survival and the toil itself. She was kind, made that
effort, she hoped, less and less but still, she tried, on and
on. As soon as Alma could wield a short-handled hoe she
bent her back to work the land. Her mother begged until
the girl was let go to school, and begged each year until
begging ceased to be effective, and after third grade (she
still couldn't quite read or write and never would) Alma
worked the dirt from daylight to dark.

Great-grandpa Cecil could not ever seem to reconcile
himself to his circumstances, or want to, and sat still more
often than could be forgiven. He'd been born to comfort
and a fair portfolio of wealth in Texas, blown his inheri-
tance before the age of twenty-five (he drank wildly and
thought he could gamble wildly, too), gone to his kin to
beseech for more, a new start, and within a year blown
that as well, then become permanently estranged from his
family when they would loan him no more, not a chance,
don't even bother to ask. His face flushed to a scalded red
that didn't go away and his hands quivered. The DeGeers
never spoke again, nor traded letters, birth or funeral no-
tices, and became unknown to each other. Being born to
poverty one is accustomed to the degradations and needi-

ness, hence at home in all that dinginess, while not much is worse (Cecil was certain of this) than becoming accustomed to a high station from birth only to watch yourself sink, incredulously, lower by the season, until you land bumpy-assed on rocky dirt with folks cloaked in rags and desperation who were now your peers, no arguing that, but who would never feel like equals. Cecil was basically unemployable by temperament; he quit jobs over slights no one else heard or even assignments stated too plainly, the very plainness of wording an insult to his pedigree. This arch sensitivity to social hierarchy prevented him from working steadily, a sullen employee always, even if he worked for himself, every workday a diminishment of his proper standing in the world, a daily lessening that meanly sapped his vim, rendered him forlorn and inert, while his women, made natural vassals by their gender, worked like swampers, muckers, field hands toiling for his ease. They sweated dry in sunlight and slept in stiffened calico. Cecil sat and dreamed or walked to Wilhoite's for a jar and returned home to resume sitting, his dreaming now aided by gulps of shine. A far richer life continued hourly behind his eyes, a life painted on sky-blue panels, and in it he was again a well-to-do DeGeer from Lampasas with daily feasts, horses to the horizon, cattle spread beyond, petticoats falling in a white drift beside any bed he rested on.

Alma fled at fifteen, sorrowful to leave Mother behind with little Ruby and that old drinking man, crying as she ran, but positive-sure she'd strangle herself before midnight with a barbed-wire strand if she didn't start running today, this minute, get to town, tear open a new life and crawl inside.

Ruby had it worse. She was allowed no schooling at all, and Cecil in his dotage had become fond of the whip. He applied lashes to both Ruby and her mother and shouted his point of view while they ducked or cowered. Despite being half-nosed and forever working, Mother stood accused of lying with strangers, probably at creekside while Cecil slept, since he'd pondered on the porch and convinced himself that pretty little Ruby must be the spawn of a fornication that had not included him. In looks she did not favor Cecil or any kin he ever saw and that made her nothing but a mouth to feed, an ass to beat, a young body of no relation he could sometimes let his hands rub on the buds and rump and linger until his breathing thickened and he had to lie down next to the whore, her mother, for a piddling relief.

It was grim living and those years made indelible memories that would never die or even fade enough to be misremembered. Flashes of recall would forever plague Ruby, those stunning jagged flashes that contain crushed feelings, certain smells, sorry pictures that fired unbidden into the mind and made her cringe, cringe, cringe, and she'd cry into her hands for an hour or go find a man she'd render weak with her smile and lead him straight to the shearing shed.

Then came the morning Cecil did not wake but

stretched purple in bed, tongue lolling, and soon enough after the farm was taken by the bank and Mother's fortitude dispersed skyward in a single beam of dimming light. She'd lost her final ounce of oomph and was moved to the Work Farm, while Ruby, at age thirteen, was sent to town and Alma's care. In very short order Alma found a live-in job for Ruby as an apprentice laundress and general helper at the home of Mr. and Mrs. J. T. Duxton, who had a large house on a good street, two teenaged sons, and plenty for a young girl to do.

M r. Arthur Glencross would eventually have a statue of his likeness placed in a position of honor on the town square. Glencross had many fine qualities and a pleasing manner he'd adopted as a teen and clung to throughout. He was born into a family of assistant merchants, that is, folks who did okay but spent their days as clerks in parlous (even torturous) proximity to those who owned the factory and did mighty damn well. The social distance between grated and Glencross was shaped early by the resentment his folks nurtured in private and shared with him in words, glances, facial expressions. He was a half-decent baseball player and an excellent student, one A+ (instead of a mere A−) shy of being valedictorian of his class. During deer season he went to a camp in the forest with his father and cronies, but he preferred fishing mountain streams alone. His only dates in high school were with daughters of his mother's close friends and none was memorable or repeated. His folks did without luxuries, scrimped and saved, and he was sent to the state university at Columbia. There he lived in a quiet rooming house of dour scholars and achieved the honor roll, heard John Cowper Powys give a lecture on the meaning of art that enlarged his mind, saw Mabel Normand wave a long-stemmed rose from a touring car, and became deeply smitten with a large and brilliant girl at Stephens College who had to be reminded of his name every time they met. Business reversals required that he return home after applying two and a half years toward a four-year degree, and he did so with hangdog reluctance but quickly took a job at Citizens' Bank.

He was a tall young man who stood at the back of crowds and blended, but Corinne Jarman spotted him kindly helping an elderly and crabby customer in bibs down the bank steps to a mule-drawn wagon and asked her father for his name. Within a month he was invited to the Jarman house for a Sunday luncheon during which he ate heartily but barely spoke. It was a spectacular room of chandeliers and crystal goblets and objets d'art that Mrs. Jarman had purchased during her second Grand Tour of the Continent. Glencross felt obliged to concentrate fully on each act of the meal so he wouldn't break any crystal or spill on the rug, spew food while speaking that stained the beautiful tablecloth. He could not proceed with such caution through the elaborate requirements of a meal so complicated and also follow the conversation flapping around him, so he missed several opportunities to engage with Corinne.

She was tiny and thin and pale as a cloud that might

be parted by a jaundiced thought. Her manners were exquisite but unforced and her eyes were compelling blue places. Each movement was as precise and fluid as those he'd seen actresses display onstage. Once the luncheon concluded she took his arm and walked with him under an umbrella into the bright garden where their courtship began when he spied a spread mimosa tree and quoted a snip from Wordsworth in response to the fragrant shade it cast. "Behold, within the leafy shade . . . on me the chance-discovered sight gleamed like a vision of delight." Corinne seemed thrilled by the attempt at poetry and he seemed nervous, suddenly concerned that he might now be expected to have an apt quote for many sights or situations and he did not.

It was difficult from the start for Glencross to accept that a local princess was truly and seriously interested in him, but he hopefully amassed a few phrases of French and read a book about table manners. He called on Corinne during a hot spell and they sat fanning themselves on the veranda where he spent all his French quips within an hour to great effect, judging by her smile, her lowered eyes, then invented on the spot much longer passages of Latinate sounds to further woo her. She seemed to believe every word she thought he'd purred to her in a Continental language and swooned. He felt masterful, nearly sophisticated, and though in the coming weeks he gave her a couple of chances to escape their involvement, to realize he was unfit for her world, she didn't take them and an engagement was announced. Before the winter holidays of that year they were married, and while on their honeymoon to New York City she spoke to him in middling French daily just to see the captured expression it brought to his face.

Their wedding gift from the Jarmans was a huge house so splendid and grand that it intimidated his own parents whenever they visited and they never would tour the entire place but kept to the parlor with their hands held clasped on their laps. But he promptly acclimated to the new facts of his life, began to dress the part, to learn how to spend money without gnawing regret at each expensive purchase, and all was fine except for this: Glencross did not know much about sex coming into marriage (he had one night experienced a few moments of mysterious fumbling of fingers and lips and buttons and belts behind the Columbia train station with a woman who needed another dollar to get home to her mother, and though something gooey had resulted between them during that dark transaction he was never certain that he'd truly lost his virginity there) and Corinne knew less. A merely awkward coupling between them was counted as an achievement, but most encounters seemed painful, perhaps degrading in several particulars, always to be conducted furtively even within the bonds of matrimony, and certainly unnecessary to the new Mrs. Glencross. She preferred to have her mind tickled intimately and to keep her clothes on. She loved Glencross but did not love his body or her own, and he never in all their years together saw her completely nude. At the birth of the second child it was as though she'd broken the tape at the end of an arduous race, and would race no more, she had her trophies. He accepted her position and did not complain, much, but adjusted his lust to the parched conditions only with the aid of considerable liquor and long fishing trips taken alone. She seldom asked him where he might be going and that worked for them both.

Within four years as an employee and one year of marriage he was boosted to become vice president of the bank. There was some muttering, of course, that his sudden wealth and in-laws had too much rigged things in his favor, but he quickly displayed talent for the demands of his profession, was sharp at calculating relevant numbers and harvest yields from any crop, tireless, and good with people, so his youth ceased to be mentioned as an obstacle and two years later he was president. (And it was good he was there, for he saved the bank during the Great Depression, all agree, held it together with sweat and personal charm, some helpful silences at key moments, but mostly hard work, inspiring confidence in depositors with his bearing and palatable grandeur—he'd still take off his fine threads and handmade shoes to go quail hunting with customers, farmer or swell, wearing ordinary clodhoppers and a cloth cap, do a little night fishing down at Gullett Lake, split a bottle of pre-Volstead scotch whisky with golfing friends. There were hundreds, including Harlan Hudkins, who believed they were personally saved from financial ruin and the Work Farm only through his business talents and integrity.) There were, however, days of coping when he silently disappeared from the bank at noon or from home after Sunday church and drove alone but for good whisky to fish the Jacks Fork, Eleven Point, Current, Twin Forks, or the Spring River on the Arkansas line.

And it was the case that Alma and Ruby did sometimes on Sundays visit Mother at the Work Farm two miles out of town. Mother no longer spoke (she would pass three months hence) but seemed to know them, and it was this sense that she yet knew them that compelled them to continue the visits even though they took all afternoon. The sisters had to walk heavily along a dusty road carrying lunch in their purses. Their step lightened on the return trip and they avoided the topic of Mother to keep it lightened. Arthur Glencross in his mud-streaked Lincoln Phaeton did, while returning fishless from a trip with an empty bottle, come upon them walking in the late glare of the day and stop to offer a ride. There was a seat beside him and a seat in back. Both women hesitated, then Ruby strode toward the passenger's door just as Alma did the same, but Ruby elbowed her way to the handle faster and held the seat tipped forward so Alma might climb in back, then slid in front. Alma glowered from the shadowed backseat toward the front and was mystified, even frightened, by her glowering and its possible source.

Glencross said, "Excuse my hat, ladies—it somehow fell in the mud."

Ruby responded, "About any ol' hat looks good on a man who knows how to wear one, and that man's you."

At the Glencross house that week Alma avoided him as much as she could, kept herself busy in other rooms, doing other chores, for she was pretty sure she knew what was coming. And it did come, in an envelope Glencross put into her hands and said, "Pass that along, won't you?"

At the Dunahew shack she and Ruby stared at the envelope and smelled its scent of vanilla and admired the fine script. They had to wait more than an hour for a child to come home and read the enclosed card to them. Sidney, nearly nine at the time, opened the envelope and read: "Dear Ruby, I have a business trip down to Mammoth Spring—would you care to take a ride into the country with me? I expect it to be this Monday. I have cleaned my hat. Say you will and tell Alma."

Reporters arrived from all across the nation and encouraged the profusion of theories and suspects, making their stories pop with color and intrigue they might not have invented entirely, but certainly in part. The first person to confess did so within a day of the blast, a fractured widow-woman named Watts who lived in the spare room of a spinster daughter and said she did it with bombs the Huns had smuggled over awhile back and hid under the Fussell Creek bridge because her son never visited her anymore and was likely dancing with men again since he was still alive and a devotee of sins that can't be spoken. The papers ran with the confession for one edition, then dropped it without further comment and listened instead to Fred Crown, a war veteran and former fireman, who said, "Only dynamite skillfully placed could have blown that building so thoroughly to bits."

The first suspects were picked by Mrs. Howard E. Tompkins, who said that those Gypsies camped beside Blue Spring (there are several Blue Springs in the region, this one being the smallest and closest to town) had threatened all citizens in no uncertain terms. Mrs. Tompkins had been suckered out of six bits and taken advantage of only two days before the disaster by dusky fortune-tellers who kept seeing into her future and predicting experiences that Mrs. Tompkins had already by-gum had; she'd long before met a sightless man in a black hat on a rainy day, had a child get cut bad but live without a scar, and found a blue egg under a laying hen that was hollow and floated like a cottonwood puff. They were seeing her past and selling it back as her future, the liars. Her husband asked Sheriff Adderly to chastise the Gypsies for charging seventy-five cents to tell his wife that her future consisted of events she'd already put behind her, and he had, a tad roughly. The boss fortune-teller, in her multihued headdress and bangles and beads, raised her index and little fingers in the sign of the horns as led away, and said, "You'll see gray skies with no stop. Gray skies spread inside your chests of bones to stay and above your heads forever. Fie on you one and all."

After the explosion that woman's dire comment was enough to suggest their involvement as a tribe in this terrible revenge, and Mrs. Tompkins made the suggestion loudly and often, even if most of the Gypsies had been locked up when the night sky turned yellow. The jail was in the courthouse, six cells on the third floor, and a mob carrying noosed ropes quickly assembled at the front door to jeer the Gypsies and threaten them with hanging or worse if they didn't come clean, admit their evil, point out the ones who'd planted the bombs. Deputy Bob Jennings said at least two of the male Gypsies let messes into their trousers when questioned with billy clubs, and the women knelt below the barred windows, keened and threw shrill prayers skyward at some greaser god he didn't recognize or care to meet. When the sheriff released the Gypsies four days later he did so after midnight and escorted their slow parade of caravans to the county line where he used a bull-whip to encourage them to move along quickly and get gone from his sight.

Sheriff Shot Adderly was a country galoot from some hopeless crossroads who'd come to town and found society pleasing and his calling as a lawman. His given name was a homemade epic, Leotozallious, but he'd been nicknamed Peashot as a teen because of his small size, the name short-ened to Shot as he matured, a substitute name he was ever so glad to have considering the one he'd been as-signed at birth. A year later, when nothing had become clear to the public and the Citizens' Commission Inquiry had been seated, Sheriff Adderly said, "If I was to tell all I know about the Arbor Dance Hall blast there'd be lynch-ings from here to St. Louie."

M r. Lawrence Meggs hung sucker-bags from trees at the edge of his yard and ate venison year-round. He had thirty acres, mostly on a slant, and a slanted garden he'd made bountiful by pushing four hundred wheelbarrow loads of barnyard dung through the creek and uphill from his neighbors' place. His folks were gone and it was all his to tend and he'd only ever gotten away from this land one time. He'd gone to Kansas City to visit cousins for a month the winter he turned nineteen. He'd been very ill at ease among so many streets and strangers, so many voices that talked another lingo, was gawky at everyday sights and un-nerved especially by the sweet and curvy temptations of the nights. At the third twilight he put his Bible on the closet shelf and laid his hat over it and his cousins' bad example soon enough put him at ease with a couple of simple sins, neither of which he had ever given up — sipping devil juice and whoring. He went to the Chesterfield Club in the middle of the day and the wait-resses there didn't wear shirts or dresses or even little aprons, but served blue plate specials bare-assed and smiling, standing with their secret hairy parts at eye level while he pointed at the menu, and he spun away from there after lunch so puffed with lust that he'd had to pay twice before teatime at Mrs. Vanatta's on Grand. He returned to the hills different and kept his mouth shut about it, mostly, but no longer felt worthy of marriage, a blessed state, his favored sins yet surging alive within him and released so regularly he dropped churchgoing so as not to be phony in God's house and only read his Bible when the weather kept him from walking to the crossroads for sunken company or into town for a dance.

Harlan explained, "It was more than the dead, boy, it was also the maiming, the ruining, breaking folks into parts that left them incomplete but still breathing. You'd see them pretty regular limping down the avenue, maybe using crutches, or trying to work with one arm at a two-armed job, buying face powder by the bucketful to hide the scarring, certain ladies always wearing knotted scarves so you might not notice there's ears missing off their heads. This town had some mighty scarred and torn citizens and we noticed them a lot 'til the next war came, when pretty soon scarred wasn't the worst that could happen to a citizen. Larry didn't have anything left to call a body but his trunk section, plus a cooked arm that dangled awful limp but could lift a cup. An aunt on his mom's side and her husband moved up from around Bull

Shoals to look after him out there. I always did like ol'
Larry just fine, you know, knew him about all his life,
but I suppose I visited him less than I ought to've done.
A lot less. In about 1935 he somehow rolled downhill
into the creek, and I was happy for him."

The Dunahews had in 1890 turned their backs from the green places, the unfurling mud of the old home, and trudged toward factory money and landless days, lured to town by a tall gray pipe puffing smoke that marbled darkly into a stoic sky, and there they soon became chained as a family to that very smokestack by a stub of pay that amounted to almost enough. Town was a fresh confusion, so many faces that would never be named or known, everything run by a congress of social power they could feel squatted on their shoulders but never see plainly or throw off, the rules of life now strayed a giant step or two sideways from the direct and bristly ways of conduct they'd known and understood in North Carolina, Kentucky, and most recently on Egypt Creek where it meets Big Chinkapin.

Grandpa Buster was born in town within weeks of the clan's arrival, and his lifelong loss of balance was expected from his birth. He was a babe that wanted six hands to pull him from the womb, his first squall a wail of horror at this eviction, a cry of dispossession that was remembered and seemed all his days to be poised near his lips for another release, another howling from the lost place inside. He became okay-looking and long, smart enough but smiling more than was required, as he was so often guessing at just what was expected of him or called for in response, hence the reflexive teeth-baring at veiled insults or insults outright, news of the weather, the war with Spain, a death in the family. He hoped to be liked by all and was easily urged by peers toward silly errors that greatly amused those who'd done the urging.

His youth was a torment of social distress and unnecessary smiles, with nothing to recommend him as a figure of worth until a posse of native teens went to the hobo camp across the rails and started a ruckus for sport, which aroused three hardened 'boes who'd fight and gave chase, and Buster, not so fleet of foot, turned when caught and threw a right-handed punch that found a chin and dropped the biggest hobo to the mud, left him there senseless. Just one punch and the man fell like a sandbag and after that jokes on Buster began turning toward the benign and affectionate or inclusive.

With no ground to plant and share the Dunahew clan fragmented by 1912 and scattered in pursuit of unlinked futures elsewhere, while Buster remained but would not seek work beneath the local smokestack, just wouldn't do it, and instead painted signs, houses, barns, as part of a crew headed by Mr. Loyce Mackay. He married Alma in January of 1916, and none too soon if yellowed birth certificates are accurate. He worked for Mackay and struggled with a dual matrimony, having become betrothed to the bottle also, a love he encountered early and fell for straightaway. It looked for all the world like he was having the highest of high old times when he'd been drinking young and gleaming, sowing oats, being a little wild, stacking empties on the windowsill, laughing too much, dancing too late, knocking a fella senseless now and then when a wild night turned mean.

There were things Alma would never tell me, and one was how she'd met Buster, a subject that made her sniffle. I used to hazard guesses, some of which offended her ("I never took a drink in my life!") and none of which ("You seen the birth papers and you can do numbers, so don't ask me that again or I'll snatch you bald-headed.") she answered. All she ever presented as a response was "I loved what there was of him. Still do."

Alma earned a pittance and combined with his pittance they got along barely until the first child joined them. As James grew and added his needs to the economic grind, Buster turned hugely patriotic overnight and sailed away with our troops to Europe, anything to get him out of the house and stark proof of his daily failings as a provider and teetotal. He had a bad go overseas with the AEF, smelled mustard gas somewhere in France, shot occasionally toward enemies he could hear but seldom saw and lost three toes to trench foot, returned to the shack with shined eyes and a shambling gait. The blue monster that has fed on almost my entire family had swallowed Buster whole before he boarded the ship for home, and possibly before he boarded the ship going over or threw that right-handed punch.

He did in his veteran funk shortly become a drop-down drunk who could many times be found on the sidewalk at sunup, a figure of torpor and ongoing disgrace his own sons had occasion to step over going to school, walking on with eyes averted while not mentioning him and hoping no one else would, either. (John Paul would during his marriage oft endure this comment and variants from Harlan Hudkins, "I recall so well seeing your daddy on the sidewalk before breakfast with spittle dried on his face, and it always made me feel so safe, so very safe, don't you know, 'cause whilst I slept comfy in a feather bed ol' Buster Dunahew was out braving the night and keeping an eye on things for all of us, keeping a lonely vigil out there without needing to be asked—it was like having a watchdog that spoke English when it was sober. I bet you felt proud.") He was evicted from the shack but often encountered around town in various ignoble postures and soaked states of mind. This went on for years, paused for pneumonia and a recuperative season in the shack, then went on for more years still. But there did come a morn in autumn of 1928 when he awoke in a wet gutter near the square and was stunned by the awesome beauty in an ordinary dawning, sunlight bursting onto window glass, clouds riffling among many colors, a bird on a wire, a dripping of oil that stretched a partial rainbow down the grimed pavement, and vowed to Glory while still supine to become temperate. He tried and shook and sweated, begged Alma to let him come home, but she had no reason to believe in his cure so soon and said, Not yet, not yet, just remember I love you. Grandpa Buster Dunahew, dry as perdition for nearly five months, died in a confusing car wreck (not his own car, but a rackety Ford on permanent loan from Arthur Glencross, for whom he secretly chauffeured) on the Eleven Point Road near Mountain View, twenty-three days before the Arbor Dance Hall blast.

Her hands ached always before she was out of her teens, joints risen, knuckles become bulbs, and it was those aching and distorted hands that she spread flat and warm on each and every of the twenty-eight caskets assembled in the high school gymnasium. There was no other site in town vast enough for a mass funeral, and even here there was an overflow out front, onto the street and into the vacant lot beyond. A long, long line of sighing mourners filed past, each casket heaped with flowers, the mass of them surrounded by framed portraits on stands, cards of farewell written in block print or intimate cursive, stuffed animals to carry along to heaven, three baseball mitts, a military helmet, a hunter's horn, a velveteen smoking jacket. Alma touched all twenty-eight and kissed them each, kneeling to kiss the fresh black paint between her spread aching hands, said the same words to accompany every kiss because there was no way to know which box of wood held Ruby, or if she rested in only one, had not been separated into parts by crushing or flames and interred in two or three, so she treated every box as though her sister was inside in parts or whole and cried to the last.

James was stony-faced and stiff, held himself to be too old for weeping and too tough, but Sidney and John Paul wailed behind Alma's skirt, tapping little fingers on the spots where she kissed, their faces crumpling and red from missing Ruby horribly already and knowing they would forever. Sidney, quiet and memorably sweet for a boy so often in want, was paled by this grief and the unsuspected disease that would take him young, and smart skinny John Paul, whose restless, insecure and angry energy would become his prime asset in life, felt drained by the end, slumped listlessly, and could cry no more.

The town was represented from high to low, the disaster spared no class or faith, cut into every neighborhood and congregation, spread sadness with an indifferent aim. The well dressed and stunned, the sincere in bibs and broken shoes, sat side by side and sang the hymns they had in common. Mrs. Glencross, with Ethan and Virginia accompanying, sat next to the Dunahews, a public gesture Alma would never forget, though Mr. Glencross remained at home, still in pain from burns he'd received trying to pull survivors out of the ruin.

Six pastors and the only priest in the region addressed the mourners, voices rising to be heard over the tidal disruption of sobs, cries, hallelujahs, and occasional shrieks. The service lasted more than four hours, time for many mourners to settle, their thoughts to stray from piety and remembrance, and when finally the crowd wandered out-side onto the sidewalk, into the street, quite a few voices blamed the deaths on a colossal accident of unfathomable origin, a test from above, while others could be heard sug-gesting earthly causes or suspects, courses of action that might remedy some of the mysteries, names of those thugs or crazies or outsiders that belonged at the top of any list. There was anger crossed with grief and nowhere to turn for answers but to those six pastors and the only priest and gossip.

The state penitentiary squatted above the Missouri River, a brick monstrosity with high red walls and guard towers, cold and wet, hot and humid by season, mean in spirit all the time. Seen through iron bars the flowing river was a constant beckoning toward escape, but the river had a savage history and accounted for a host of resolute cons who'd drowned while briefly free and fleeing across the hungry brown water. Discipline inside the walls aped the medieval, with prisoners clubbed by guards or lashed at a whim—for making eye contact or not making eye con-tact, for slouching like a hoodlum or standing insolently straight, because they talked back or wouldn't answer at all—bats on the head regularly applied to encourage order or unconsciousness. The seriously disobedient were hung from chains in a damp basement room, feet held inches from the floor, tortured slowly by gravity, and as joints began to sag free from sockets screams reached into the cells above and alerted all who might misbehave to the meticulous agony that awaited them downstairs. It was a general population of tush hogs from the hills and bullies from the avenues, asshole bandits and free-world queers, snitches who sweated fear in their brains and tier-bosses who dreamed plans for vast empires of vice that might be made if ever they walked unshackled in sunlight again. The pen was a famously brutal place that released more brutes than it received, and sent them home changed beyond easy understanding or tolerance. Jack rollers and bank robbers, pimps and yegg men, some ready killers, some ready enough, returned to their villages or clusters of tenements with bitterly gained knowledge of meanness and the hollowing at their core that allowed them to employ it in any way that felt good at the time, which was mostly right now, this minute, on the spot.

The Arbor Dance Hall occupied a huge open room (the building had originally been a yellow-brick dairy barn) above an automobile garage, the ground level a dim space for mechanical repairs, new tires, or for men to stand around jawing with other men. It was operated by a gent known as Freddy Poltz who'd been Walter "Plug" Reinemann once, a tough who'd made a few mistakes on the streets of St. Louis, done his time, and upon release picked himself a fresh name from among the graves of his mother's family in Borromeo Cemetery. As Plug Reinemann he'd been muscle for Egan's Rats, shadowing Willie Egan himself as various gangland spats erupted, Jellyroll Hogan getting greedy, the Green Ones or Cuckoos trying to expand, dagoes off the boat and stray Hoosiers agitating all over. In 1921 he'd been lighting a cigar at Fourteenth and Franklin when Willie was assassinated, falling and standing, falling and standing again, then falling flat as a cop rushed over and asked if he'd say who shot him, and between bursts of blood from his mouth Willie replied, "Naw, I'm a good sport."

Plug saw the future in Willie's dying eyes and decided to avoid it by getting arrested per arrangement with the chief of detectives—nothing too serious, just a few years away for a robbery he had indeed committed—so Jellyroll and the others might forget his face, forget several things he'd done to earn his nickname while running with Willie. But in the passage of those few years in stir Plug slowly grew toward the available light and became aware of an astounding interior truth—he actually hated tough guys with their dullard insistence on petty tributes and gaudy hats worn at an angle, despised them, hated their humorless jokes and gleeful violence, maybe always had loathed them at a subterranean level even as he carried out their orders, and he would seek their company no more. Tough guys, once pondered in a quieted mind, were revealed to be boring, really, just so tediously dangerous and boring! As Freddy Poltz he amassed for himself an innocuous history as a commonplace rustic who'd done no notable wrongs or rights anyplace, ever. He married a sunny woman in the sticks who didn't know his real name until he died in the blast, and had two children who after his passing felt timid and unmoored the remainder of their lives. His wife, Mae, worked as a cook and laundress for Mr. and Mrs. Edward Williams over on Curry Street. She was a regular on the bench outside the Greek's, where every maid in town came to know and admire her seriousness of intent and casual charity.

The unraveling of Freddy Poltz began when the leaves were down. A fog bank low to ground lapped the skin on the mud to a treacherous slickness, and two eight-man football teams banged away at each other on sliding feet in that field beside the old high school where the Methodist church sits now. The leather ball disappeared into the huddling gray sky whenever punted, leading to entertaining miscalculations by stumbling players staring skyward who could only guess where the booted thing might squirt from the cloud and slipping off their heedless feet as they shifted directions to make a catch.

The teams churned the field of blanched autumn grass into a thin flat wallow and drew an audience with their animated voices. The small crowd was free with suggestions on how players might want to improve and were disputed from the scrum in return. At game's end Freddy was exhausted, spattered by mud to the distance of his hair, and alarmed by a face beneath a brim hat that stared his way from the center of the crowd. He looked at the face and the face kept looking back. Freddy quickly said his so-longs and left the mud and the face followed. Freddy walked directly across the railroad tracks and took the path under the Fussell Creek bridge, where he stopped in the shadow, turned around, "What do you want?"

"You're Plug, ain't you? From Egan's?"

"Not lately."

"Who is it you are now, Plug?"

"A decent man, and I'm stayin' him, too. So let's us promise to not be seein' each other again, Mikey."

"Can't make that promise, Plug—or Freddy—I hear you're Freddy these days—might make myself into a goddam liar, and how's Mother goin' to feel if word I'm a goddam liar gets back to Kerry Patch?"

"So you're still in the game."

"It's the only game that tickles me right."

"Well, I don't tickle no more, so leave me out. Just leave me the hell out of everything you might get up to—am I bein' clear?"

"Okay, okay, don't get in a huff. Just wanted to say hello 'cause I knew you when you was up to no good in the city, and here I go scoutin' the boondocks—and this is sure 'nough the boondocks, brother, nothin' but brush apes eatin' dingleberries and draggin' their squaws by the hair—when I see a city face from home to talk at, so I do that. Listen, I got no kick with you, we're still pals, far as I care. But Humbert and Jellyroll and them, they wouldn't call you pal. No, Mr. Poltz, I don't think so. I don't think they ever will. Not after what you done on Ashley Street that time."

"What's your bite?"

"Nothin'. I don't want nothin', not really. Only, say if people who know people you know dropped by while passin' through here, solid people scoutin' for safes and things like that, could you help them all they want? I think you should."

Freddy walked home by a looping, indirect route and pulled the shades, told Mae and the kids he was going fishing of a sudden and might be away two or three days, but don't worry if it's more. He had no pistols, only a shotgun for taking game birds, a hefty double-barreled he'd never fired, and when he grabbed it dusty from the closet beside the bed, Mae asked, "What kind of fish is that for?"

"I might want to eat meat."

"Why bother with the fish, then?"

"See you."

He returned in three days, clean-shaven, wearing new clothes, with no fish and no meat. During the coming weeks his personality began to warp and erode; behavior she'd become accustomed to from him was now unconvincing or gone, his regular good cheer replaced by pacing about with a narrowing face and glancing from the windows. Her singing irritated him at any hour and he'd bark he wanted more gravy on his potatoes from now on and other days bark for not so much. He let the children climb onto him and play but did not join the play, seemed not to note them on his lap or clung to his leg or otherwise seeking his attention. He quit football on Saturdays and ate less. His sleep had stories in it that he mumbled in jags until certain scenes shouted him upright. After his death, she found among his personal effects inside a bottom drawer a folded edition of the *Scroll* reporting the big news that a dead man had been discovered in a clearing at Saunders Camp, beside the Twin Forks River. The victim had been shot until his face scattered beyond identification, the only clue to his name or origins a brim hat with a tag inside that read, Selz Fine Clothing, Carr Street, St. Louis, Mo.

Mr. Isaiah Willard was a jackleg preacher, a man of hard convictions walked up from Little Rock after he'd walked from several places before that. His preaching was not deeply rooted in the styling of any single church and had a rough angry tone, accusatory subject matter, sparks and ash flying from his mouth. He cast out plenty who had blackened spots on their souls and argued or would not tithe. He offered an unforgiving response to those who failed to accept his rendering of Scripture into a parched syllabus of sacrifice and toil, pain at unpredictable intervals but guaranteed, then death in the ground and a life eternal above if you'd minded his teachings to the end, hell if you hadn't.

His church changed names and angles as he'd walked

the nation, and here it was known simply as the Tree of Christ, housed in a small white storage shed at the southern edge of town. There were still a few tools leaning in a corner, half a sack of feed and a torn washtub, but he attracted a flock of seven who liked to be chastised by a stranger and raked across the coals. As his influence over the seven grew his preaching ranged about and added features that some would call vindictive, purely and simply, once they thought it over, but his flock doubled as these ranting subplots attracted those locals who dearly craved wrath.

There were so many acts or thoughts or mere thoughts of acts that could plant rot in a person and choke the flow of the blessed spirit until the soul became wizened and shrunken and fell away from the body, useless as a dry booger, and a soulless body was but a hospitable husk soon become filled by a demon. The soul of the damned was now a dry booger on the ground somewhere and the newly resident demon shielded behind the face of the husk laughed and laughed, threw stones at stained-glass windows, made babies sick, mothers die, pestilence abound. Preacher Willard accepted the Ten Commandments as a halfhearted start but kept adding amendments until the number of sins he couldn't countenance was beyond memorization. He appeared to be adding new ones shaped to your own reported shortcomings until you were tailored appropriately for a residence in hell, and nowhere else, but a complete and prostrate begging of God and an increased tithe might, just might, earn you one more chance at heaven, who knows, give it a try, it's only money.

Among the easiest portals to the soul through which demons might enter was that opened by dancing feet. Evil music, evil feet, salacious sliding and the disgusting embraces dancing excused provided an avenue of damnation that could be readily seen and blockaded. Through the spring of 1929 Willard and his knotty flock protested the Arbor Dance Hall. Those young decadent fools upstairs shook their bodies all about in thrall to impudent music, smoked cigarettes in mixed groups on the sidewalk, and from the alley a spill of devil juice scented the entire ugly picture. He reared back with the Book raised overhead and preached blue peril on the street outside until revelers began to mock him from the high windows, then from the street while walking past him with their promiscuous hands wandering one another. The top of Preacher Willard's head unscrewed and hovered out of reach when derided by these gathered sinners with their smug hedonism and flouncy garb, and before the start of summer he said in a mighty letter of epic frustration printed in the newspaper, "I'll blow this place to Kingdom soon and drop these sinners into the boiling pitch—see how they dance then!"

At least twice a night little brother pissed into a milk bottle and I marked the yellow-depth on the glass with a green crayon. He'd wake me when he had to go, and it was my job to then block him from the bathroom, holding him, threatening, sitting on his back if called for, until I could hear a convincing trill of pain in his voice, then hand him the milk bottle. We were trying to stretch his bladder so he'd have no more accidents. We slept three boys to a room, triple bunk beds with one lowered, but older brother was busy with his increasingly adult dreams (this was not quite a full year before he married at seventeen and moved to the basement with his younger bride), so I'd take the warmed bottle out to empty it in the toilet. Dad would often be at the kitchen table, beer cans beside his textbooks, a smoky cloud of scholarship hung between the table and the light. He used a church key as a bookmark and always wore white shirts (such attire meant something deep to him that I never needed to ask about), dress shirts for work, old dress shirts for daily life around the house, mowing the lawn, leaning over a fence to joke with neighbors, chasing the bums who stole milk off our porch. Dad was a drinking man who worked all day selling metal in St. Louis, came home, had a couple of beers (Mom's greatest domestic victory was when she convinced him to forgo scotch whisky except for the most special of occasions and stick to beer otherwise) and a ham sandwich, then drove back across the river to attend Washington University on the G.I. Bill. He was a dedicated student at night and never missed a day of work.

He'd look up at me carrying that piss bottle in the wee hours and say something like, "Had economics class tonight, Alek—I learned that if you're going to steal, you should steal a lot." Or, "Have to read a whole goddam novel about baseball, only it's not really about baseball, see, it's about sad-assed stuff I already know all I need to know about, but there will be a test."

The house was a dinky box on a street of dinky boxes, with two bedrooms, one small, the other smaller. When visiting from West Table, which she began to do after the summer I had with her, Alma slept at the far end of the kitchen on an army surplus folding cot. The reconciliation with my dad seemed to have dismissed her focus, and she began to float languidly among her own pliant thoughts. Alma was almost hourly becoming less anchored to the day she was living and twirled into and out of days gone by or days she'd imagined. She often addressed us boys by the wrong names and I would answer to any of them, but the others wouldn't, and an expression of agonized confusion would slacken her features as the correct names bounded into the summer weeds and hid from her.

The house was mostly a riot by day. Mom worked till noon answering phones at St. Joe's Hospital, and with Mom gone we boys ran amok—blasted the Animals, Chuck Berry, *Hot Rod Hootenanny*—bounced fat rubber balls off the ceiling, interrupted others on our party line to call grocery stores that had Prince Albert in a can, stuck darts in windowsills, closet doors, upholstery or flesh, brought in neighbor kids and beat hell out of each other for practice—while Alma would go into Mom's kitchen and demonstrate her superior domestic expertise; put the pots and pans here instead of there, move the plates higher on the shelves, set the skillets under the sink, stack the canned goods differently, rethink the entire knife, fork, spoon drawer. Mom would come home and again spend an hour of her day mumbling and putting everything back into place, then lie on the front room floor with a wet cloth over her eyes. For two or three days Alma would overlook the disorder in the kitchen, the poor strategy employed by her silly daughter-in-law, then fix it all once more.

Dad was in a rough spot between Alma and Mom, and it was made rougher by Alma's deep suspicion that strange men came to the kitchen window and looked in on her at night as she changed for bed. These men were usually silent, but she could hear them breathing when the wind was right, and see beams from their flashlights lashing the walls. She would throw grumpy little tantrums in the evenings, vent her fear through the early TV programs, and Dad would on several occasions finally have to go out back and watch for perverts so she could get into her sleeping gown. I would sit with him. Two metal lawn chairs were set in a good vantage point, and Dad and me would watch and snicker, then catch ourselves and say it wasn't funny. Or at least not the kind of funny we should be laughing about.

Headlights cresting the slope on the next street over played briefly on the window nearest to the cot and bled through slits between the curtains. She'd sometimes part a curtain suddenly and stare about for culprits, then withdraw. A big twin-trunked cottonwood tree blocked the moon. The houses had been built so cheek-by-jowl that in warm weather we could hear conversations, snores, sometimes farts or lovemaking from inside houses in two directions.

"Why won't you talk about Ruby?"

"When you're older."

"But something wrong happened, Dad—don't you care?"

He'd light a cigarette, raise a beer can, mutter scraps of sentences he avoided pulling together. He'd watch smoke trickle toward the sky until the muttering ceased and he spoke coherently again: "She sent me home a little agitator, didn't she? A goddam protester. If it isn't Ruby with you, it's taking up for those bums sleeping by the river who steal our milk. Why is that?"

"I know them, is all."

"She got hold of you too young and gave you a hard twist in the head, got you facing the wrong way. That's my fault."

"All I do is ask questions."

"Look, Fidel, listen to me good—you've got to learn you can't go around being angry at everybody out there who has a swimming pool or a shiny car—that attitude won't work very well in this ol' world. Takes you nowhere. Those fancy-pants sorts are the people have to hire you someday—they can tell if you hate them in general."

Alma's sad furtive undressing continued, with a few peeks between curtains, then the light went out. Fireflies signified all around our yard. There was the scent of cut grass, a slight stench of motor oil and gasoline, honeysuckle. Somebody's mother called impatiently across the dark to bring in the children from the street behind. Dad smelled of beer and the warm smell of beer has always made me feel hugged and home.

"I will say this much; if it wasn't for him, I'd've never gotten to here, gotten to someplace that didn't know who I'd been born as and would give me a goddam chance, let me fight for some of the pie, at least. I lived through the war for this, son. A chance. We needed help getting away from home the year you were born, you know, *sick,* and I needed to leave to find a decent-paying job, and Harlan wouldn't offer. Not a dime, not a dollar. You know how he is about his money. Glencross gave it, though, without me even asking. I bet she never told you that."

He didn't know what he truly liked between the sheets until she showed him. She saw inklings of his desires in his eyes, sifted through his bashful talk and long silences and deciphered what wasn't said, then delivered those mute cravings onto his novice body. He had spasms he thought holy in nature and in her embrace could have them again more quickly than he'd ever believed possible. She knew all the worthwhile crevices and wrinkles and bulbous places that made the body entire sing and sing of release, and the more release he experienced the more he sought. Her lips were fine on his, so learned, and her hands moved over him like those of a necromancer delivering a resurrection, for she raised him up with fingertip touches and her fragrant breath and pink caresses. She probed him while lying on quickly spotted sheets in ways he tried to halt, but didn't quite, then didn't try, then asked for again. She took him to places inside a shaded room that he'd only dimly imagined might exist, and while there in sweaty reality he reclined like a pasha of lust, a man lost to squirts, sighs, fresh angles of entry and the enveloping stink, and to find this carnal enchantment for the first time at his age was to welcome a streaking of madness into his life—madness he prayed had no end now that it had begun.

The Burton family brought the very first piano to West Table in 1883, ordered out of Cincinnati and delivered from the railway station by ox-drawn wagon, but no one in town knew how to play it until their youngest daughter was born and taught herself the rudiments. In time she had her own daughter, a sweetheart named Lucille Johnston, who was by age eleven a local prodigy, a little blond girl bent reverently over the keys releasing waves of grace with her tiny fingertips. By seventh grade Lucille began spending a fortnight of her summers studying with the best available pianists in Springfield, usually, but upon graduation she did also experience an eye-opening month in Chicago. Back home again she supplied chaste and stately music at church affairs and civic affairs, but at house parties attended by quite different flocks would let her hair down and bang those eighty-eights until the girls danced barefoot and the men had to go sit on the porch to cool down.

At age nineteen she said, "I swan, I swan," at a so-so joke and realized she had fallen in love with Ollie Guthrie. Her parents approved. She and Ollie both beamed during those dreamy weeks of engagement as if permanently amazed at the repeated wonders that took place daily between two hearts so opened and well matched. He gave her a ring and a necklace with a heavy brooch that she wore more than she did the ring, because the ring was too valuable to risk losing and she had to remove it to play. The couple were to visit his mother's people out at Rover, but the regular Arbor pianist had been stranded in Cape Girardeau, and Lucille reluctantly agreed to sit in with the house band so the dance could proceed and her friends could frolic. Ollie sat on a windowsill watching her with a smile that never wilted. The explosion sent them in different directions, and three days later he identified Lucille by the brooch that had burned deeply into her chest.

She has washed his shirts clean of her sister for months now, scrutinized collars, cuffs, taken a hard block of lye soap to lipstick smudges, and scrubbed away that smell the girl splashed on and the smell of him and her rutted into a smell that could not be mistaken by any wife for another.

("You need to stop puttin' on that perfume."

"But he bought it for me. They like you to wear things they bought you."

"It catches on his shirts and lays a high smell in there."

"He likes it."

"I have to wash the stink out, though, and it ain't easy."

"That fragrance is imported!")

In the wind of every season she aired his jackets on the line, ofttimes for two days or more. She washed his shirts clean of her sister and aired his jackets pure and turned a blind eye toward intimate caresses in the backseat of a rackety Ford pulled to the curb out front and the scarlet joy that on some nights set Ruby dancing merrily in the shack. It was a mess of wrongness she just had to take, she knew her place, and had three sons with stomachs pinging. Glencross eventually noticed how discreet and effective she was in keeping knowledge of the affair from reaching his wife through sight or scent, and began to covertly press dollar bills on her almost weekly. He never stated a reason for the increase in pay and didn't need to, either— she caught his drift plain and clear and accepted the bonus dollars with a quick twisting of two or three confusions inside her chest.

("Are the both of you in love now?"

"We're somethin', sister."

"Somethin' what, though?"

"Somethin' that's the berries, sis, call it any name you want, but it's runnin' mighty sweet, and I can't see where it'll stop."

"It had ought to stop now."

"He has this way of layin' there eyein' me all sleepy with just a tiny bit of his tongue poked out that reaches to my toes and curls 'em back . . . and . . . you see what I'm sayin'?"

"Oh, I hope you never do make her know.")

On days spaced two weeks apart she would accompany Mrs. Glencross to the office of Dr. Thomason on Jefferson Avenue and sit in the shadowed waiting room while treatment was received. He was perhaps the oldest doctor in town and continued to apply remedies to women that most doctors had in recent years phased out of their practices. Noises that Alma could not associate with the practice of medicine did many times reach her ears through the walls as she sat and tried not to hear the intimate whimpers and grunts or comprehend too clearly when she did. Mrs. Glencross required the administration of rejuvenating paroxysms every fortnight and drank elixirs in tiny sips on all other days, rain or shine, but still she was wan and routinely lacked pep. The lady required Alma at her side to brace her upright as she sagged from the relief afforded by medically induced shudderings of the pelvis and remained loosened in her limbs on the return walk home.

"I'll hold your umbrella up, ma'am."

"Thank you, dear. My health, it's as it has ever been."

"Did the doctorin' treatment go good?"

"I prefer you not pry, Mrs. Dunahew. I do appreciate your arm to lean on, always, but don't pry."

The congregated silhouettes of ruin attracted steady visitors who arrived most evenings around sunset to stand and behold in the everyday wonder of sinking light just what contortions tragedy had wrought and left in view. Remains of wall torn to fractions still somehow stood here and there to make partial and keening shapes in the gloaming. Dogs had for a time gathered on the spot in snorting packs, but the siren stench of rot from the pit had finally wavered and blown away. Burned wood, sprung wires, shanks of cloth, bits from scarves and hats and handbags and crushed shoes were sifted among the tumbled bricks and blackened debris. Rainwater stagnated at the bottom of the pit and made muck beneath returned chunks of the scattered building.

Sheriff Shot Adderly did his rounds there at that hour whenever he could and observed. There were regulars in grief and tourist connoisseurs of the tragic and regulars again. Some knelt in prayer, some recounted news of their day on this earth in an intimate babble of words directed to the crater, and others stood at the edge and

gazed upward, seeking a flashed revelation in the twilight. Arthur Glencross now and then arrived in finery
to stand at the edge and look down and only down
toward the dank and jumbled mess. He seldom stood
there for long, but might arrive in any weather and ig-
nore it, foul or fair, and stare always with such emphasis
that his presence was felt and eyes were drawn toward
his figure.

Adderly again and again approached him slowly and at-
tempted a conversation along these lines, "Somethin' here
draws us back over and over, don't you think?"

"Something does indeed."

"Say? How's that burn scar of yours doin' these days?"

"That's three times you've asked that, Shot."

"And three times you don't answer."

"Good evening."

Preacher Isaiah Willard did on occasion arrive at the
pit to spear those assembled in hurt with flung condem-
nation, blaming the dead and their damnable desires for
their own deaths, bellowing that the gospel truth was now
made obvious to even the blind and most unrepentant
among them—sin here and sin there if you please, fools,
but know God's wrath will find you even as you jerk about
to pagan sounds and bounce reveling in said wickedness.
They who perished here in a sudden burst only received
that which had been earned by them, yea, verily, by their
own will and wicked ways, and... Shot Adderly did twice
warn Willard that forbearance in regards to this broad loss

mightn't be the chief virtue of the citizenry hereabouts, and as he understood it the Lord didn't hate polite silence altogether, and Willard gave his retort, which was, In the face of idolatry and sloth and sin He does. Don't tell me He doesn't, as when others sleep I hear Him direct while alone in darkest hours, and remain fearless in His embrace and at His command.

Leo Adderly, Jr., Shot's middle child, on the thirtieth anniversary of the Arbor Dance Hall blast, said to a sophomore daughter who reported it in *Ridgepath,* the student magazine, "Papa, in secret, had a real dislike for being ordered around by the big cheeses in our midst. Told to say something wrong was really okay because the drunk kid came from a good family, or the silverware thief was an important so-and-so's wife, all that run of thing. About half of what a sheriff does is to bend laws a little to keep the right people *out* of jail—he knew that from the start, and it's an elected job. He generally bent the law when he had to bend it, Papa was not slow thinking, but on the dance hall deal he intended to settle that hash so honest and direct there'd be no doubts left about what was what, who was who, where the blame fell. He wouldn't let himself be turned left if the trail turned right, not by anybody, and if he had to leave town after he'd got the truth, he'd leave, and leave well pleased. I'd guess he was awful pesky to deal with. Of course he didn't get to see it through. And the main thing he ever said about the whole deal was that he'd been at a meeting in an office above the square, and had three or four of the biggest cheeses suggest to him that he back off, look somewhere else and don't find nothing. He said they put it to him just this straight: 'Some calamities are best left unexplained, Sheriff. Aren't the fish biting on the Twin Forks?'"

Buster Dunahew did when flush smoke Helmar Turkish cigarettes. (Most of his days he'd resorted to discarded butts of any make found on the floor, sidewalk, barroom ashtrays, sometimes shadowed on the street those citizens who favored his brand and graciously littered.) He stood in the vacant lot across from the rental cabin at the Current River ferry, leaning against a blackish Model T sedan, and lit a virgin factory smoke. He always tried to park far enough away that he wouldn't hear his sister-in-law moan and yip, groan and succumb, talk dirty or tell lies. This cabin was a favorite, and the pole-driven, rope-pulled, one-man ferry across the Current was seldom in heavy use. Forest erupted springtime-green rose unbroken on the slopes to a high vee, and blocked from view all but a split of blue sky and the river. The water had a clarity that would in afternoon light allow Buster to admire his face on the surface and see through himself to count individual rocks on the riverbed.

The cabin was built of raw wood from trees felled nearby, sawed into wide planks and pegged into place neither varnished nor rubbed altogether free of curled shavings or splinters. The pioneer roughness of the cabin oddly gave it considerable appeal as a love nest. The bed was near to ground with a fat mattress and the dabbling pan sat on the dresser. Ruby dragged the sponge from the pan under her arms and through her pungent narrows, smiled his way, said, "Okay, yup, I do like their hats. But it's their shoes give me shivers. People notice shoes. You think it's rings or necklaces or maybe just eyes—but it's shoes that make 'em look close and get a first idea of you."

"I'll give shoes some thought."

Ruby came bedside and knelt, laid the sponge onto him where it mattered and rubbed. "Can't have her catchin' my smell left on you."

"She won't smell it there."

"It might soak into your britches."

"She won't there, either."

"Maybe I just like washin' you."

"I didn't say stop."

Buster sober and alone had to regrow his life from the dirt up, and it was a harrowing process but a solemn duty, too, rising from flat on his face to his knees, to standing, to standing upright and walking on with a lessening wobble to his stride. Different clothes helped, gave him a different posture. He became straighter and taller when resplendent in a cloth cap from Galway, tweed jacket, flannel slacks—in return for secret chauffeuring he received favors from Mr. Glencross, whose greatest favor of all was to share Buster's height and waist size and to quickly tire of excellent clothes. Buster in recent times wore fine and sporty threads with labels from New York, London, Boston and Havana. Glencross sometimes teased him with the aroma of scotch whisky (a political figure supplied him with Teacher's Highland Cream by the case throughout the years of Prohibition) raised and passed beneath his nose, sometimes teased too much and meanly appealed to Buster's gross familiarity with defeat, but otherwise they got along swell and there were the woven benefits that fit so well and modest tips in cash. Glencross could not have his Lincoln Phaeton seen parked in front of country hotels, highway motor courts, cabins at the river, and under no imaginable circumstances would it be proper for Ruby DeGeer to be seen alone in his company—any scandal provoked by his Phaeton being noticed where it ought not be, or even whispering of a possible scandal might cripple or sink a banker in a town so small, and he found his public ease now at no other level but the heights and was not willing to fall.

During the week before the Arbor Dance Hall blast, Alma pleaded with Ruby in the shack to drop this new fella and return to Glencross, he kept weeping so in empty rooms and neglecting business, disrupting his own household with sadness and unaddressed odd talk. Buster's drunken death was yet so ugly and fresh and she craved calm, calm, why won't you see Arthur Glencross loves you as best he can? Ruby sat listening with her shoulders down but hopped up with eyes averted and with a weak toss sent her last hat toward the nearest wall. It fell short and went down limp as a harvested dove. She said, "This will be sorry news to hear, sister, and I didn't want to say it, not ever say it for you to hear, but it'll give you the answer you're huntin'": Buster would not drink. He would not drink and drove very carefully on those slender bumpy backroads, eased over sections that had washed out and become rolling wrinkles of dirt or eroded to a steep tilt that required he drive at a slant. Glencross sometimes had one too many and other parts of who he truly was inside slipped out and went on display. He liked to taunt folks just a little bit when pie-eyed. He and Ruby were riding in the back so they could duck from sight when ducking was required, and he opened the second bottle for another slug of scotch he didn't need. They came across two grinning kids with switches and a mutt driving hogs to the sale barn at Mountain View and that slowed them. The weather was fine, all kinds of sky and not cold or hot. It was called Eleven Point Road and only lightly stamped into the dirt and narrowly snaked those leaning hillsides. The kids used switches and the mutt to part the hogs at the next wide spot and Buster picked a way through. The bigger boy trotted beside the window and asked, "How fast will she go?"

"Fast enough to get me there."

"Bare feet'll get you there, mister."

"Not as fast."

"Show us how fast, would you?"

They needed to make time back to town and came up fast and honking behind an old man in a mule-drawn wagon who didn't pull aside but gave them looks over his shoulder that hinted he did not much respect the assumed dominance of automobiles on the road or those modernized people who did. Glencross said to pass the sonofabitch but there was no room and Buster said so.

"Pass that sonofabitch."

"There's no room."

"Maybe if you had just one tiny drink you'd get the nerve up to pass that sonofabitch."

"There's no room."

"Here, perhaps a mere smell of this will do the trick."

"Get that away—I don't drink—hold on to your hats back there."

The road-mud skirting broke away beneath the wheels when Buster drove wide to pass and dropped them down-slope to the south. The car slammed along with tires touching ground to bounce and ended as part of a tree with the hood crushed upward almost straight and Buster wasn't moving. The steering wheel pushed into his chest. Released dashboard pieces, sprung seats, dust and personal items scrambled about inside the car or flew out. The motor ticked and wheezed and wheels spun and creaked. The windshield showed green leaves and blue sky behind cracked glass and Buster's blood had reached the cracks to flow them as tracings. He made sounds but did not speak or move.

Ruby had a broken left forearm and bruises on her neck and brow, but rolled from the backseat onto weeds. Gasoline smell was strong and spreading. Glencross heaved in his chest and hacked blood and phlegm but joined her in the weeds. When he could stand he looked in on Buster. You could see the future cross the banker's mind and scare him cold. He saw tomorrow forget his name and title and stroll past him without so much as a fond glance his way, and dulled years ahead living faded from wealth, and didn't care a bit for the depleted sights or sensations. Blood leaked onto his own coat and shirt collar from his nose. He went down to his knees at the car aimed up and reached under for the bottle of scotch and carried it to the steering wheel where he sprinkled whisky over Buster, whose eyes moved his way and blinked. Buster impaled was sloshed by whisky he craved in anguish every day but denied to himself of late in his strengthening pursuit of benediction, and weakened horribly as the homing smell gathered and rose about him. Glencross pulled Ruby to her feet, and said, "We've got to get to West Table."

"What about Buster?"

"He's a goner and we aren't. I can't be caught here."

"He's not dead."

"They'll smell him and that will be that. I can't be caught here."

"We need to find help."

"There's no help around anywhere near—look at that old man drive those mules away. Think he's going for help?"

"I think he might be."

"I can't be caught here—coming?"

And Ruby did so state to her sister that she considered running, gave thought to fleeing Buster as he died, but something in her center came awake and she saw...she had not suspected him to be this brute bigwig now revealed in alarm before her, but understood on the instant that he was, he was, and felt sickened in a manner she'd never been sickened before. She reported, "Everything about him said it. If one more of us was gone forever in a crash he considered that not much lost. He left me, too. East Side dirty-leg. Everything about him...we just don't mean spit where it counts."

She did alone and with pain crawl back into the Ford, gas smell or no, and raised her working arm to touch her fingers to Buster, on the face, the shoulder. She stroked his hair murmuring whatever noises bubbled up, whispered the same, and he watched clear sky dimming through the bloody cracks and no help arrived for almost five hours. He was dead after one. She touched him for two, woke on the grass and weeds when somber kids with switches and a mutt returned leading adults carrying lanterns. In sleep she had stiffened. She couldn't swing her left arm or stand unaided. The next day Glencross said to her immediately after a plaster cast had been applied at the Bogan Hospital on Osage Street, "I did what I did for us, Ruby."

"You never."

"What earthly good would it do for me to lose everything—he would've died anyway."

And Ruby said to her sister, "There's no way to love that in a man."

The second crucial event that urged Charles Lathrop to ruin was sparked on the seventh day of June, 1933, when he came awake in his home down Bois D'Arc Street and smelled betrayal wafting from his wife's pillow. This scent of betrayal took the form of barbershop pomade, a richly scented, thickly poured pomade, pomade that had been transferred to his wife, surely while writhing in an illicit embrace, from her to her pillow, then, during the bright hours of that morning, into Lathrop's mind.

His wife, July, who had been born a Powell and was as pretty as all local Powell girls seemed to be, said something to him, but afterwards she was never sure what. Good morning, honey. Eggs sound okay? Sure is sunny out.

Whatever she said received no response from Lathrop. He pulled on a sloppy set of clothes, clothes for doing messy chores, then dragged a white rocking chair out back of the house. He used the old ladle at the old well, pumped himself a dipper of water, then positioned the rocker among the grapevines his father had cultivated in what was by then Lathrop's backyard. He placed the chair so that the vines closed in to render him invisible. He drank a bucket of well water that morning from the well his people had been drinking from since the War Between the States quieted. Lathrop had just turned thirty-one, and remained childless after nearly six years of marriage. His job was secure. He owned the house outright. But on that date in June he sat strangely in that white rocker behind the vines, drank well water from an old ladle, and howled. At several points he let loose with howls of anguish that neighbors recalled for years to come.

Just as the factory whistle announced the noon hour, Lathrop rose from the rocker, walked into the house he'd been born in, on back to the master bedroom and a chestnut dresser that stood against the south wall between the windows. He bent to the bottom drawer, pulled it open and removed a ball of chamois cloth. From the cloth he extracted a large pistol of obscure make and placed it inside a pocket of his trousers. He then selected a black rain slicker from his closet. The slicker fell low enough to hide the pistol butt hanging from his pocket.

He said several things to July, who never forgot them or disputed them and repeated them but twice, then walked out the front door and onto the sidewalk, taking stiff deliberate strides toward the town square. He turned west on Main Street where tall, wide trees shaded his passing. At the mouth of an alley that joined Main he passed the lean-to made of ill-fitted lumber known as the Clubhouse, where hardscrabble men drank and gambled at dice and cards or checkers while waiting to be hired for day work. Several of those men said they noted Lathrop, and that he exhibited "a strange wander to his eyes," and walked like he was roped and being pulled by a mule to somewhere he didn't really want to go.

Lathrop went on past Clellon's Billiards, where he made no impression, then the Raleigh Hotel, where a man named Pence standing on the veranda said howdy to him and received a curt wave of acknowledgment. Lathrop entered the square on the east side. As he threaded through the lunch-hour foot traffic he nodded absently to several people who would later that day dearly wish they'd touched his arm to pause and spoken with him. Halfway around he exited the square and continued downhill and north on the avenue.

He walked several paces in that direction, then slipped into an unkempt alleyway behind the shops and stores. He came to the back entrance of the old Winslow Stables, which had been only partially converted to an automobile garage. There remained soaked inside those walls strong lingering aromas of horse sweat and liniment and horse apples that melded with the up-to-date stench from oil and gas. Tommy Uphaus worked in the bay attempting to repair either an old Republic truck or an older Apperson Jack Rabbit, he wasn't sure which upon reflection, but he did turn when Lathrop addressed him in a soft polite voice: "John Teague around?"

"Not now."

"When will he be?"

"He's off on business today."

"Won't be in at all?"

"I can't think of why he would be."

For reasons he could never articulate, not at the time or decades later, Uphaus stepped completely away from his work into the alley, watching Charles Lathrop wearing a rain slicker disappear beneath clear sky toward the railroad tracks.

Lathrop did soon after on that day become our first suicide (three others are certain) called by clarion misery to the dance hall site. The pit had finally been filled in earlier that year, the debris and sadness removed from view, the pit filled with dirt and smoothed level. Mrs. Henry Easthall watched Lathrop from close by, on the tracks where she walked hunting sassafras that might be growing to one side or the other, and said he had the pistol in his hand and spun around, paced irregular circles a few times, then went still at just about the center of the new dirt. He saw her watching and made an apparent statement to her but with intonations more appropriate to a question, so maybe it was, she never could decide: "It's all gone flat since?"

During those years in which Alma DeGeer Dunahew was considered to have become crazy, her brain turned to diseased meat by the unchecked spread of suspicion amidst a white simmering and reckless hostility, a caustic sickness between her ears could be witnessed by viewing the erosion of the very color in her eyes as she raged and the involuntary sideways tug of her lips as each heated word was thrown.

Folks said, "Grief has chomped on her like wolves do a calf."

For some long seasons she was by spoken edict deemed unemployable among the finer families of West Table, once they'd tired of her bottom-dog scorn and wide accusations aimed generally upwards. She had on a bright gusty morning been summoned to the front parlor by Mrs. Glencross, who asked her to sit, and as Alma sat her eyes went to her remaining chores—the pale pleated curtains hung over windows often raised open to wind and blown dirt, their stylish dainty pleats making so much unnecessary trouble for Alma, the silly things, requiring that she part them gently to shoo dust and tiny black specks from the many, many whitish crevices, but not parted so much that they stretched ugly and remained gaped—and Mrs. Glencross went on about something in her level voice, no rises or dives in tone to alert one that she was getting to the serious point or points. There was a hallway rug of Persian design that needed beating in the yard, today or tomorrow, and on the post at the foot of the stairs waited the sinuous brass stem and glass globe of the Vapo-Cresolene lamp that must be lit at the arrival of every dusk to combat those pernicious poisons that ranged in darkened air and harmed children most—when she caught an odd note of finality, "That's all. You've worked your last hour here. I know what you said at the Citizens' Commission, Mrs. Dunahew, and it was shameful. I cannot have you in my house anymore."

(Mr. J. William Etchieson, cochairman of the Citizens' Commission Inquiry, to Alma Dunahew on the stand: "Are you aware that Dr. Thomason has testified that he personally treated Mr. Glencross for burns?"

Alma: "I figured as much."

"He treated him with salves and ointments repeatedly."

"I saw him come over repeatedly, and I saw the ittybitty hole in the arm he treated, too—it might have hurt plenty for a couple of days, but it surely weren't no kind of burn."

"Dr. Thomason noted that it was a small burn in scope but acute, and he managed to minimize the scarring."

"There never was no salve or nothing of the like on the bandages I took out to the rubbish after he come over, though, and done his treating. None of that yellow mess that you spread on burns, or the red kind, either. Only sometimes a little old spot of blood, and that only on the first visits.")

"They told me whatever testifyin' I had to say would be held secret."

"Yes, well."

"So them official muckety-mucks all amount to liars, too."

"I believe you have cracked from so much woe, but even cracked you surely know he had not a thing to do with the tragedy. Not a thing."

"I know what I know, ma'am, and there ain't no way to not know it now."

"You've been snooping in my home ever since...I realize that...and we have been so very kind to you, always, haven't we?"

Alma stood, dismissed, fingered her hair into place, and stared fixedly toward the staircase, then as she departed said over her shoulder, "Ma'am? You'll want the long kitchen matches to light that lamp."

She found occasional day work available in the more modest homes of other victims, sympathetic families who were also suspicious of various people but chose to stay silent in the face of enormous evil. Alma could not tolerate even sympathetic cowards for long, fearful that close contact with the surrendered might by example draw her own spirit into a puny presentation of itself, and to keep her spirit stout she did at times talk aloud about the silent and surrendered with mocking inflections as they sat inside the room she presently cleaned, sorting them out in understandable slurs as they paled, then reddened, and amidst the responding babble she'd leave their employ in the next flushing seconds, broom dropped to the floor, laundry washed but not hung on the line, and walk directly to the pit the explosion rendered. There she would bend at the waist and shriek her terrors downward past the scorched debris and brick wreckage to the mucked bottom and beyond, where she needed most to be heard.

Folks said, "Alma believes she knows why and who but can't do a thing—which is a black curse for a body to carry no matter how you say it."

She let her hair grow too long for kitchen work by simple forgetfulness, her mind had been trained elsewhere for so many weeks and months, but when she took notice of the new length in a restroom mirror decided on the spot to let it grow on forever, having an immediate hallowed sense that hair of an otherworldly length displayed a public, devotional reverence for the dead, for the dead and her quest to achieve for certain of the dead justice or blood, one or both, but especially both. Her clothes had never been special and now they were grimed by neglect and the upchucked spatter absorbed by plain cotton print as she tended a dying son who could hold nothing much down.

She had no steady job and all kinds of miseries, and folks avoided her or became briefly blind when she walked past on the square with hair sprayed about her head neither combed nor bound. When so shunned she many times would follow closely on the heels of those who chose not to see her and whisper or deliver in singsong approximate injunctions from the Bible: "Masters share onto your servants that what's A-OK and fair, hear?"

Or: "The righteous fallseth seven times and is rose up standin' at scratch again by rooster-crow tomorrow—what do you think about them apples?"

Or: "The tongue of the just is chose as be silver, and ain't none of you got tongues of silver."

The fallen, though, would still give her work, and Alma did at times swab and scrub inside establishments she would not have entered before, lowly and vile joints wherein neither her attitude nor station were held against her, and sweeping was sweeping and a bowl of stew and corn bread could carry a soul. These brigands and outcasts and assorted whores were sinners, yes, of the gravest kind, but they feared not the opinions of the highfalutin that held sway in this town about themselves or others. Alma pinched together what earnings she could from Cozy Grove and the Willows and Aunt Dot's, and at Jupiter Grocery laid grubbed coins on the counter to again secure the smallest fatty ham hock, an onion and more navy beans for the boys.

John Paul would take to sleeping outside the shack on

those nights Sidney scratched most horribly after air and tried to inhale deeply but came up shallow. His straining chest and thin bones rattled like chains born far apart inside him that clanked together now as he emptied. Leukemia, no remedy but prayer, and don't count on prayer to be heard when broadcast from this room in this shack during this mean year of our Lord. (John Paul would never again attend church nor pray privately from the time Sidney's sickness accelerated through the completion of his own.) Sidney lay on an uneven cob mattress in the center of the floor, eyes shrunk to slits or suddenly drawn too far open, skin the color of spilled milk disappearing into a slow creek. John Paul wept and held on to Sidney's feet to warm him. Wept and laid a wet cloth on the fevered forehead to cool him. Wept and ran outside to flee his brother's rattling chains and the strangling stink and kept running. Alma tended her dying boy as well as she could with only a mother's hands and beans in pork fat and no special medicine of any kind. James paced on these clenched nights from wall to wall and front to back and smacked himself in the face. He opened and closed his Barlow knife as he paced. He smacked and opened and closed and at times, as if whispering to a nearby cohort, repeated, "You're right. You're right." Sidney lay among kin where he'd laid for weeks with ebbing breath and did not ask anymore for food or a cure, but stared up with resigning eyes and asked the ceiling or whatever to let him go, C'mon, just let me go, go now, go soon, go.

He robbed banks. He called himself Irish Flannigan, a blatant falsehood and redundancy, as his true name was not Flannigan but Bosworth, and he was only guessing that he might be a pint or two Irish on his mother's side. She was always nattering to him about their forebears and one time or another suggested that a dab of this or a dab of that from nearly every white-race bloodline of the world had been introduced into his veins, so he could claim kinship with just about everybody in charge if it somehow got him a leg up. It would be as Irish Flannigan that he achieved a bright but fleeting notoriety, became for a glorious time loved, feared, hated, idolized. He and the Irish Flannigan Gang robbed more banks in the breadbasket than any of his permanently famous brethren ever did— Pretty Boy, Dillinger, Machine Gun, Baby Face, the Barkers. He outrobbed them all, but somehow his deeds never clung to the national narrative of that era, never got much publicity in the big magazines back east or newsreels, and near the end of his life he groused to his guards and chaplain often about obvious unfairness in the dispersal of fame and that pure-dee boondocks boys like himself from any field of endeavor seldom if ever received the recognition their attainments merited. He always did know such things were stacked tilted toward sating the pet wants of the citified and precious, never truly forgot that, but still, in his all-American heart he couldn't keep from... Eventually the chaplain arranged for a reporter from the *KC Star* to visit the outlaw footnote in Jeff City as his death day neared and listen while he spoke. Irish said many things that made it into the newspaper, the salient section of the article being this, "I come out of Protem, Missouri, hungry, hungry as the rest, I guess. Maybe just a little bit more. I done what I done. I won't say I didn't. I knocked over so many banks I count 'em in tens, and that number is three. I spent it when I had it, brother, danced with every girl worth dancing with and stuffed my gut with the best eats, too. I had fun. I did kill them I confessed to killing. I never wanted to kill none, none at all, but folks turn daffy on you sometimes, of a sudden think they've been sprung from a comic strip or radio show and get their dumb heinies shot. Those things I done, okay, but I never did kill no sheriff in West Table down there. That wasn't me. It was the late Eldon Haines from Tulsa. We both of us sat in the same car, I'll give you that. The sheriff they had down there was too friendly. Just too gol-durn friendly. We was stopped at a garage waiting on new tires and he come over to the car smiling, looking down to the plates, which were Georgia plates. He cozied up to the window and asked if we ever had been on the Oconee River, and Eldon cut him down. Cut him down right there in the alley before the old tires was switched with new, two shots, then stepped out and popped an extra one in his head. I want it known by all I never done a thing to the man except not see it coming."

At age ten John Paul Dunahew was on his own and raided gardens for supper after midnight. He'd been without all other kin since the twelfth of November when Alma became bizarre beyond civic tolerance and was taken to live at the Work Farm (Sidney had very recently completed his haunting, brutal, audibly and visibly grotesque death inside the Dunahew shack, James had carried away only a Barlow knife with a bent blade and stolen gloves as he fled the region), and he chased anything that resulted in coins, delivered two of the three daily newspapers (*Locator* mornings, *Scroll* afternoons) and both of the weeklies (*Gazette, Journal*) and kept his few belongings (schoolbooks, a Big Chief tablet of paper with pencil stub, two sets of underwear made from grass-bleached flour sack, another shirt made of the same, and a big wooden spoon) in a burlap bag. The Work Farm expected him to supply four bits a week toward his mother's upkeep and he did so and delivered it on foot, though he was seldom allowed to visit privately with her as she was not currently resident within her skin and they weren't sure who or what was. He could

not then and would not ever seem able to rest or sit idle—
rest was dangerous for the poor, he knew that, too many
thoughts of ordained and burgeoning unworthiness came
to the impoverished when idle and ruined them thoroughly from the inside out. He knew that before he could
say it and made himself stay on the move even when there
was no place worthwhile to go. He rose in darkness (all my
childhood and after he sat smoking Pall Malls on the back
stoop and drinking instant coffee before the sun arrived)
and hustled at any task that promised payment. He applied
to caddy at the country club but was discouraged because
of his size, and in a matter of only days became the evening
rack boy at Clellon's Billiards when old reformed Mr.
Clellon realized that he was Buster-the-drunk's youngest
son. Poker games were allowed upstairs, moon and home-
brew beer were sold from the cloakroom on the main
floor, and the sheriff never came inside the place while
wearing his badge. John Paul earned two cents a rack, and
learned to say Good shot, Nice combination, or Great
shape on that one, without looking up from whatever
book or magazine he was reading at the moment. In short
order he came to be considered something of a mascot by
the sporting gents of town. (I did once, when rambling the
nighthawk realm underage in marine green, encounter a
table of deeply wrinkled and gin-blossomed ancients who
heard my surname and ordered me a double whisky without asking if I'd take a drink before launching into fond
windy reveries of Clellon's and Clellon, Grandpa Buster

and Dad.) Many times he received tips of two or four bits from country rakes who knew his circumstances, but more often he was stiffed by those who felt two cents a rack was generosity enough. Clellon was a heaped and rounded man who theatrically overlooked John Paul's presence every night at closing time and locked him inside as though he believed the place empty, allowing the boy to sleep in safety beneath the three-cushion billiard table nearest the stove. He'd been nine, then, still, and felt protected by the apparent goodwill of the dubious. In the morning Clellon would open the front door and say, "How'd you get in here before me?" He would then count the pickled pigs' feet in the jar on the counter by the cash box, count the pickled eggs in their jar, and sometimes make an announcement along these lines, "I wouldn't eat more than three of each of them pickled things a day, myself. More'n that many a day and the brine'll tan your stomach-sack into stiff leather, and leather ain't what a fella wants down there when settin' on the throne of a mornin' to shed night soil." He almost always brought a bologna sandwich and an apple from home wrapped in newspaper and would set that lunch in front of John Paul as the sun spread early light. "Now, you deliver all them papers, kid, but don't forget school or I'll go cut me a hickory switch."

Unmothered for now and alone, John Paul would not allow himself to slide from school and sink beneath his struggles, but attended almost every day. Classrooms and study meant escape as his coltish mind was sent wandering the world by books and sharp teachers, and that wandering was in those days his chief pleasure and the classroom his place of fullest relief. John Paul enjoyed lining up to fight at Bunker Hill, Gettysburg, exploring the woods of America with Lewis and Clark, traipsing beside a belled brown cow through fragrant meadows high in the Swiss Alps, or following candlelight flickers along secret cobwebbed passageways found underneath all great castles and foreign cities.

Closely after John Paul turned ten, Mr. Clellon was dropped by a gigantic pain in his chest and buried in rain. The dug earth graveside diminished in the deluge and leaked downhill as the preacher from his wife's church spoke, the piled dirt lessening as mud with each word, so the service was abrupt and the shoveling started early. John Paul watched Mr. Clellon disappear beneath shoveled glop and felt hated by the sky and trees and rain. He owed some big shot somebody from an earlier life, he guessed, or he'd eaten a biscuit sitting in the outhouse and thus fed and nourished the Devil and God saw him chewing and won't let it go. He'd done something worth punishing, that was proved by ever-mounting evidence, but...

John Paul kept four dollars and seventy-three cents in a drawstring Bull Durham tobacco sack and had no place indoors to sleep. His various jobs provided him with one dollar and sixty-five cents a week, out of which he paid for Alma, lightly fed himself, mostly lemon drop candy and raisin bread, and tried to save at least twenty cents. He wandered the town by night, sometimes slept beside the old shack now boarded tight and abandoned or under the loading dock behind the Scroll Building. He stood at the back entrance of the Two-Way Café or the Stockman's or Dr. Bach's Pharmacy and Soda Fountain for handouts and did at times receive edible offerings from each. He was one evening near the train depot tackled by a pair of men wearing those drab wool jackets issued by the CCC, who took the Bull Durham sack from his hands, then tossed him over a wooden fence when he followed them yelling. He received in that skirmish a gash that angled through his left eyebrow and gave him a scar some ladies later said added just enough intrigue to his looks.

He took to raiding gardens in full darkness, and no summer meal was sweeter than one so gained fresh from warm dirt and still alive in the mouth. A favorite patch to plunder, easy as butter, and not far from the square, was a very large and immaculate garden and clutch of fruit trees maintained by a comically mustached old man called the Rooshian. He spoke greenhorn English with a slow suspenseful drag as he searched for the proper shaping to give words he'd already started to speak. At times he would be heard declaiming loudly in gobbledygook about irksome concerns of some sort, to which only his wife could listen with comprehension. The Rooshian's house at the north side of the garden was squat and cloaked in shadow by freely spread nature, vines sized thin to burly, with meshed tendrils and shoots, climbed over windows and up the walls to the roof, where tree limbs cluttered closely above and a skim of moss had settled on the shingles. He knew how to grow anything our climate and soil permitted and his crops were beautifully made beneath the sun and abundant.

The fence around this plenty was three rusty strands of barbed wire that had been stretched by several seasons of po' boy raids and sagged deeply between tilted posts. Even a little kid could hop through at the sagged places. Even a little kid lugging tomatoes or corncobs could hop over running away. A little kid carrying too much might not hop high enough, though, and John Paul was hooked by a barb on the top strand and swung to hang upside down. The plunder fell away from him and he shrieked as the skin of his left calf slowly tore and lowered him by the shriek. His shrieks carried in the still night. The Rooshian came to his door and stood with a spot of lamplight glowing behind him while holding a fat book open with a finger inserted to mark his place.

He made a disagreeable noise and bent to light a lantern, then came into the yard following that light through the cultivated rows and rows of green things that had leaves and rustled and dirt that lay turned and soft underfoot. The moon was no help. He wore bib overalls without a shirt and bent to John Paul at the far fence line and held the lamp close. A patch of flesh was coming off the boy's leg and had only a thin attachment to one rusty barb remaining.

"Don't you now move, huh? Fence push in still." He reached near the tearing yet snagged flesh and suddenly grabbed the sliver of skin and pinched the boy clear. A shriek, more blood. "Best hurt fast that way, boy."

John Paul in lantern light did see a white wad of himself stuck to barbed wire and the sight of his own meat hanging there doubled the pain. (Baby brother and me, when rug rats, sat at Dad's feet often to play our fingers across the irregularly shaped but smooth expanse that never grew skin to ooh and ahh over the creepy silken feel and make him repeat the story.) He was carried inside and eased onto a kitchen chair. The wife clucked and shook her head and went to work on the blood and the wound. John Paul in a strange kitchen of strange smells watched the bandage take on his own splashed color.

The Rooshian was Venyamin Alekseyevich Cherenko. (Dad misunderstood the Russian naming tradition and thought the big whoop was the patronymic in the middle and tagged me at birth with Alekseyevich. Mom argued and argued that carrying such a name during the Cold War would be a great burden, but the name became mine and I've never wished for another.) His wife was Masha, small and light, and from the first she seemed pleased to tend John Paul and renewed by his presence.

Mr. Cherenko said that night, "This garden for me and the woman to eat, yes? Yes? But we don't wish hunger on none, boy. Hunger not mischief, we feed. Hunger you got, boy. Not mischief. We wish hunger on none."

John Paul was fed heavy dark bread and a soured sort of soup that was then exotic and challenging to him but would become a favorite, and carried to a back room, laid in a small brass bed with the shape of another relaxed into the mattress. Cherenko stood over the wounded boy and opened his arms to indicate the space. "Our son lived. War came, he goes, there's cross stuck in dirt over somewhere don't mean to us nothing. Settle here, boy, to sleep. Go goodnight."

And from that moment John Paul, with no real discussion of the matter or concern about legalities, did stay with the Cherenkos as a replacement son, lived with them for years until his own war arrived and called him abroad, staying on there even after Alma was in 1938 deemed well enough to be hired away from the Work Farm by July Teague, and came back into the neighborhood of his life.

Mae Poltz and her children were run from town within weeks of the blast when Freddy's true name and past became known. A city boy called Plug who'd served Egan's Rats and rented the building had to be somehow involved, that's the sort of senseless devilment men like him were wont to amuse themselves with when uncaged, but his wife kept her lip buttoned and couldn't be coaxed to repeat the rhyme nor reason of the horror and make a clean breast of it. She claimed ignorance, and never wavered from her claim, but that much ignorance of the man she'd married and shared her midnights with had to be willful, just had to be, nothing else rang true, and she and her toddler brood were escorted to the train depot on a day of bleating weather and given tickets to a whistle-stop in central Kansas.

"If ever you think about coming back—think on it some more and don't."

When the Second Citizens' Commission Inquiry was called (after months of agitation from motivated pests named Dr. and Mrs. Mark Shelton, Haven McCandless,

Bud and Frieda Johnston, Ted Steinkuhler, July Powell Teague, and Alma DeGeer Dunahew) and scheduled for December ninth of 1941 (never held, never rescheduled) in order to deal with long-dormant but revived anger concerning still-unanswered questions and haunting rumors of provable guilt that were again reaching critical mass, Mae (now Mae Claar) was found in Fort Collins, Colorado, and asked to return. Her response suggested the commission members were out of their cotton-picking minds if they thought she'd willingly return, but she added, "We all know who it was got seen running the wrong way that night. When she blew up, everybody in town who could run did run to the fire and help except this one tall man in a white shirt and necktie, who when the sky got bright was seen by two housewives at the least and one maid and one old doctor jumping over fences and running real desperate through backyards going the exact opposite way from all the rest. Why is it we never have heard from him?"

The second summer after the blast, in the flat meadow across Howl Creek where the Skateboard Park is now, a Saturday baseball game was in progress in midafternoon, and one of the Heaton brothers hit a homer that rolled between distant saplings and down the bank into the creek bed. Two barefoot squirts on hand watching were sent to retrieve the ball and came back fast, without it.

"Where's the ball?"

"Somebody's down there."

"So what?"

"His head is not on him right and he's got his face stuck in the water."

Both teams and all three spectators made quick time to the bluff above the creek for a look. Several voices said He's dead, he's dead, he's got to be dead laying that way. A center fielder in his middle teens named Jack Gutermuth stepped to the brink, squinted downward and announced, "That's that preacher."

"Which preacher?"

"The one that said my uncle deserved to be roasted alive 'cause he could dance."

"That's him?"

"Yup."

"Well, I reckon he's in a red handcart to hell by now, about to get fried up good in his own grease—he'll keep—it's only the seventh inning."

When Sheriff Adderly and Deputy Bob Jennings arrived postgame they shooed everybody back from the creek bank so they could study the situation closely. They wandered around on all sides of the body, squatted to their heels and turned the face up. One large whitish rock had left its outline impressed in mud short of the water's edge and come to rest bloodstained and brain-spattered in a trickle near the body. The skull had been crushed and made almost triangular.

Deputy Jennings said, "There's a word for what happened to that rock, there."

"Lifted?"

"No, a better word."

"Heaved?"

"Not that one, either."

"Dislodged?"

"That's it. That's the one I like for this—dislodged."

"So, the way you suss this scene—Preacher Willard stumbled over a root or something else up there, tumbled all accidental down to here and dislodged this big ol' rock with his head?"

(Fifteen years later, Vance Bullington, who'd lost a boy and a girl at the Arbor, did on what he thought was his deathbed but wasn't quite say to his surviving daughter, Billie, "That preacher with the big mouth? In nineteen and thirty-one? I'm who done for him."

"I always have heard you most likely were who did that, Daddy."

"You have?"

"So has everybody."

"He was hunkered in the crick, there, catchin' crawdads with ham fat on a string, and . . . I'll take full credit for that killing now, I guess."

"You already have the credit, Daddy, everywhere but in the newspapers."

Billie added, "Daddy was a purty big gol-danged liar sometimes, told me he could fly airplanes backwards using hand mirrors and had once set up light housekeeping with Mata Hari over by Poplar Bluff 'til she got to boring him silly with her nosy questions, and a bunch of horsefeathers along those lines, so take his confession or leave it. I personally think this once Daddy spoke true. I kind of hope he did.")

"That's how I read it, Sheriff. That there's way too big of a rock to dislodge with your head, you know, and walk away after."

"So it's just that simple—Preacher tripped up there on somethin' I don't see and dislodged too big of a rock down here with his head."

"And died."

"Do I hear an amen?"

And there were the anniversary confessions. In the first decade after the conflagration perhaps a dozen complete or merely suggestive confessions were taken, all easily refuted, and the confessed would be returned to homes where relatives dealing with the Great Depression promised to watch over their lonesome addled kin and spend more time with them on Sundays if they could manage it, though it seemed nearly to blaspheme basic heavenly intentions to feed crazy folks when sane ones went about starving. Two of the more eager confessors were next-door neighbors who became perennials and their testimonies expanded in competition over the years into picaresque recitations of unforgivable guilt and delicious subplots of scurrilous intrigue everybody heard in detail one way or another, and plenty came to look forward to hearing yearly the advances delivered as both men tried anew to talk themselves into being hanged before the other. When one neighbor in 1937 drank raw milk too late and died, the other did sadly resign himself to not ever being hanged by others and gave up all confessing.

And there were the accusations and denunciations also delivered in clusters surrounding the anniversary date: Chuck always has liked fire too much to be left alone any-place with matches but might have been on that day— I don't got any way to know for a fact, I was at Jam Up Cave, myself, that night, but his eyes sure get wide seeing flames. Or: She and him had been stealing from the factory payroll, I'm pretty sure of that, since they had patent-leather shoes a little too rich and shiny for East Side, don't you know, and ate hunks of beef meat when we had greens and fatback, so they likely did the bombing to throw attention away from their own wrongs until they could leave for California with the loot, which they did do within only a year or so. Or: My husband has been odd since maybe a week before then, could've been a month, and if I ask him since to do things around the house when he's sitting in his chair, he won't even look up at me but says in this deep scary voice suspicious kinds of stuff, like, If I put a dynamite bomb under the kitchen table maybe you'd leave me be a minute while I read this book, which is a horrible way...

I wore Ruby's hat whenever I played Robin Hood. I found the hat in Alma's dresser drawer and promptly saw the swashbuckling potential: It was green and narrow, peaked along the center line, edged with a thin black cuff—the cuff was clearly embroidered for girls with tiny sorts of flowers, but I dismissed them as blooms in my mind and considered them rapier nicks—holding a long reddish feather that leaned backwards. Robin Hood was my top idol (rivaled only by Little Joe Cartwright, Bob Gibson and Francis Marion, the Swamp Fox) and I would open Alma's entrance to the Teagues' main house when I thought it empty and leap about from chair to davenport to ottoman, waving my sword, hurdling coffee tables and low antiques. I slid dashingly in socks across the hardwood floor and didn't break too many things. The house was a massive Victorian and it didn't seem like small things I broke while resisting tyranny in this room or that room or one of the others would be missed anytime soon.

July Teague knocked one afternoon on Alma's door when Alma napped and called me into the main parlor.

She was still beautiful, had been and would be so at every stage of life, even a boy knew that when in her presence he faced a blessed beauty, and she dressed nifty, always, since she knew she was watched for flaws wherever she went. I looked up at her with her red lips and big smashing eyes and elegant hair and confessed with a tremble before she even asked if I'd done anything wrong, and she began laughing.

"You're lucky you're one of the cute kind of Dunahew boys, know it?"

"Yes, Mrs. Teague."

"Cute boys shouldn't ever admit they know it—that peels the shine right off the cute. And call me July, please. I've told you that umpteen times."

"Aye, aye, July."

" 'Aye, aye'?—what ship were you on, sailor?"

"I haven't been on any, yet. Dad was, though."

"I know your daddy, Alek. I knew your daddy's daddy when I saw him, and your mom's people, too." Mr. John Teague owned three car dealerships in different Ozarks towns and they owned more than one house and he was not in this house more than in any other, seemed to much prefer the log place on the Jacks Fork River, but was as nice to us when home as she was. July drank bottled beer in the kitchen with the curtains drawn and smoked cigarettes on the side porch behind the honeysuckle trellis and did both with natural-born style and obvious pleasure. I enjoyed watching her do anything, because she did everything the way you hoped to see it done. She played cribbage and mah-jongg with the ladies afternoons at the country club, golfed and swam in the pool there, and her skin tanned to a fetching glow. I didn't quite get what the big deal about girls was yet, specifically, and July was older by a long stretch than my mother, still she gave me feelings I didn't recognize or know where to put. "That's actually why I asked you out here, sailor. I hadn't noticed the broken things yet—thanks for folding so easily, and confessing and all, I appreciate that, but don't break any more of my things or I'll paddle your behind. That was Harlan and Rosalee on the phone a minute ago. They want Alma to bring you by tomorrow for lunch."

"Okay, I'll tell her."

"I can carry you over there on my way to the club, if she'd like."

"She'll want to walk, no matter how hot."

"You're right. You are so right—jeez, don't you just love that old battle-ax?"

No place in town was too far to walk and Alma took me there. She delivered me to the door but wouldn't come inside and wasn't begged to do so, either. She sat waiting in the yard under the shade trees on the bench beside the horseshoe pit. Hudkins smelled of old and fresh cigars and decades of breakfast bacon, and I surrendered to the embracing smells about two steps inside the door. It was the merged aromas of lives well led, of warmth and permanence, air flavored further with gun oil and lavender perfume by a hard-nosed old sportsman and Ma-ma, who admired things English, read one or two novels daily, and put artworks on the walls depicting ladies in plumped and layered dresses standing in the garden among spread flowers and cubist hedges, overdressed and bewigged gents in blue coats or red assembled in serious purpose around maps on a table, and hushed views of the Lake District at dawn.

Grandpa Harlan took me to his paneled den and made me slap-box a couple of friendly rounds with him as usual, then look at his newly acquired and mighty handsome maple-stocked twenty-gauge he pulled from the gun cabinet and had me hold and aim. He put me in a headlock and rubbed a soft Dutch rub, pinched two knuckles around my nose and squeezed out a buffalo nickel, gave me a slurp from his can of beer. We went to the dining table when called. Ma-ma had dragged out the heavy black skillet and served pork chops fried with white pan gravy over mashed potatoes, crowder peas and pole beans, blackberry cobbler with a scoop of vanilla for dessert. On the plate it looked to be more than I could eat but I ate it all and almost asked for more. That day it was as ever at Hudkins a slow, wonderful meal, with prickly banter and quick lunging shifts of subject matter, droll jokes, rolled eyes, and laughter. Harlan and Ma-ma took me to the door once the dishes were cleared and said next summer I'd stay with them in my own bedroom and ride the horses all day, every day, any day I wanted.

Maybe a block away from Hudkins, trudging in the smothering heat, Alma, pink-skinned and sweating gushes, asked what Harlan had had to say about her behind her back this time. "He didn't say anything," I said. Fingers jumped to my ear and yanked until I could feel it about to rip from my head. "Except you're batty as a loon!"

"I knew he would."

"Arthur was his very good friend, his personal pal, and loaned him bank money every spring to stock enough feed at the mill, and did so much for folks around here. He saved the bank when thousands of others went under."

"That's no reason to look away if he does wrong."

"He said it was a horrible jumbo accident, or maybe it wasn't such an accident, we'll never know, not all the answers, and don't waste my summer worrying about old-timey sad stuff."

"Which one of us is it sounds to be worse off in the head to you now, Alek?"

Early on an amiable and improvised Saturday morning in autumn, I was with Dad at the Woolworth's located in the business section of Main Street. He was sitting in a booth drinking coffee with a man who'd once been our neighbor two doors down, but who couldn't control his jealous temper when he drank and he drank buckets on weekends. He poured concrete and made good money during the warm months. His wife was Mom's best friend and he'd tried to kill her with a switchblade knife in our front yard, got the tip into her one time, high on the arm, before Dad brought him to ground with a baseball bat. Dad whacked him behind the knee, kicked the blade from his hand, then busted him but good when he crawled toward the knife. The man was oh so guilty and admitted it every day and lived now in a rented room above Olmert's Newsstand across Main from where we sat. He wanted to thank Dad for keeping his wife alive and him out of prison, some men wouldn't have, and he hoped to find a way to win her back and live again with her and the kids, which could never happen if Dad hadn't whipped him quiet that day. He would always be grateful. They drank a few cups of coffee while I twirled on my stool at the lunch counter and sipped butterscotch shake through a straw.

We left the man at the door and walked away from the businesses and on down Main, which was a street made of ruddled bricks that rose and dipped beneath traveling tires and dated from long ago, after both the Spanish and French quit this land and it became American. Old imported-looking row houses with wood gutters or no gutters lined both sides and were rank and ailing places of begrimed brick, with rough folks leaning in the historical doorways or sitting on ruined chairs at the curb to watch traffic jitter past. The Missouri River flowed sixty yards from the street, and there was a small crotchety tavern on the corner with walls that had settled a touch out of plumb during a dozen floods and was the oldest watering hole on this side of the river. Dad said, "Let's pop in a minute— I've got to take the edge off that joe some."

We sat at the bar. Sunlight leaked in through rectangular windows at the front and shoved in through the glass half of the back door. Dad had a Stag. Within three sips he knew the barmaid's name was Rita, and he said his friends called him John Paul, and next time she used his name to ask if he wanted another. She lingered near us, relentlessly drying one washed beer mug with a white cloth, and the four or five moony morning tipplers down the rail observed this eager abandonment and were dashed in their wishful thinking.

On Dad's second Stag two bums came to the back door and opened it to speak. "Rita? Could we get us those beers?" They were heavily powdered on their faces and hands with black dust. It had rained the night before so they'd slept out back in the giant coalbin by the tracks because the bin had a roof and the piled coal held them above ground high from the swooshing water. They hadn't yet had a morning rinse at the spigot by the depot.

She said, "Did you pick it all up already?"

"You can look if you want, 'cause we did."

I slid from my seat at the bar and approached the doorway and said, "Hiya, Bill. Hey, Speed."

Bill stood dusted black in bright light and looked closely to see me in shadow, then said, "It's Derby Street."

Speed said, "Have I ever had any trouble with you?"

"No," I said.

"Keep it that way, then."

"He's the Russky kid from Derby Street."

"Well, now, the Russkies was our allies in a pincher movement when it was good news for me and everybody crossin' the Rhine they was, boy, I'll tell you."

"He's the one brings potato chips in a great big can sometimes."

"That's my favorite kind."

Rita carried them two beers apiece and they both grabbed one in each hand and turned away. I knew they'd head to the thicket visible through the door, where in reasonable weather or foul in desperation, bunches of them lived hidden away along narrow trails curling between the tracks and the river. She said, "See you Monday, gentlemen. You're on your own tomorrow."

Dad stared steadily at me once I returned to the stool and sat. He lit a smoke without need of a single glance at the pack or the lighter, created a gallop from his fingernails tapping the bar, and his eyes didn't leave my face. "You know those characters *by name?*"

"Sure. That's Bill and Speed."

"I heard you twice the first time, son. Why do they call ol' Freddy the Freeloader, there, Speed?"

" 'Cause when, like, teenagers and stuff drive around here they like to slow down and call bums over to their car and ask for directions or something else to get them close, then squirt shaving cream or throw rotten stuff or dog flops in their faces and laugh and drive away, but Speed can catch them in traffic at the stop signs."

"He can, huh?"

"Bill says Speed is the fastest bum alive."

"When he catches them, then what?"

"He'll whip up on them a little, or at least try to, no matter how many are in the car, and he gets bloodied and kicked around pretty bad sometimes, too, but they likely won't be quick to ask him for directions again."

"I don't know if I want you knowing those sorts too well, son."

"Dad, Bill and Speed aren't the ones who steal our milk—don't you ever even once in a while wonder about Grandpa Buster?"

"No."

"Never?"

"Your grandpa Buster was a bum."

"Just because you're a bum, it doesn't mean you're bad."

"You're right, son. It doesn't. I stand corrected. It absolutely does mean you're a bum, though." He tossed a few dollars on the bar and scooped his cigarettes, left the change. Rita said, Come back soon, John Paul, and he winked like he might and led me to the door and out. He squinted in the sunlight, yawned, stretched, yawned. "I've got two goddam tests coming this week—Modern Business Theory and Shakespeare, and Shakespeare's the one I'm worried about."

"We haven't got to him yet."

"That flowery fart has things to say, but he sure doesn't make it easy to get what he means." We walked along the old warped street toward our wheels and paused to stare at the river when we were between buildings and could see the water and all the way across to the next thicket. "But when you do get it, it was worth the trouble." Dad slid into the Mercury wagon on his side and me on mine. It started right up at the turn of the key, which was an only occasional result, and we pulled into traffic to drive six blocks up Derby Street to home. At the first stop sign Dad paused with his foot on the brakes and stared ahead in reverie down the uneven bricks of Main. "I think I like Speed."

Trains have haunted the nights in West Table since 1883 and disrupt sleep and taunt those awakened. The trains beating past toward the fabled beyond, the sound of each wheel-thump singing, You're going nowhere, you're going nowhere, and these wheels are, they are, they are going far from where you lie listening in your smallness and will still lie small at dawn after they are gone from hearing, rolling on singing along twin rails over the next hill and down and up over the next onward to those milk-and-honey environs where motion pictures happen for real and history is made and large dashing lives you won't lead or even witness are lived.

On the cold night of November 10, 1933, James Dunahew hid inside the Glencross garage, knife drawn and opened, blowing on his hands for warmth, cap pulled low, listening to repetitive mockery from the goddam singing trains. When Arthur Glencross arrived home late he did not park inside the garage but left the car on the driveway and turned toward the front steps. James rushed from the garage back door. Glencross began to woozily turn to the sound of movement and James tripped the man, shoved him onto his back and fell upon him, stabbed his blade high in the body. He stabbed twice and Glencross looked up into his face and said, "Oh." The man did not resist past the sighed "Oh," and James shoved his small blade through the heavy overcoat a third time and the blade bent. He had intended to become a murderer this night but recoiled when engaged in the act, repulsed by the feeling in his hands and the forlorn grunts from his own chest and the shock delivered him by Glencross's abject acceptance of the assault. There was no blood visible on the coat. James never said a word, but withdrew his blade and started to stand, then dropped again and pulled the black leather gloves from the wounded man's hands. He raised upright and looked at Glencross where he lay, pulled the gloves on and nodded one time, then ran toward the singing rails, boots stomped on the street with loosened soles flapping, breaths gray as ash tossed into the air behind, and was gone from this town forever.

Two days later Alma came unstuck and wailed to pieces in public. Glencross received fourteen stitches at the Bogan Hospital and told Sheriff Bob Jennings that he'd been cut by two pasty-faced men with severe northern accents who'd driven away in a white coupe he'd never seen before, but he told Alma the truth and she broke. She broke and yawped accusations at the town in general and the gentry by surname and released blanket lamentations for all the needlessly dead during one full day and most of a morning. That knife in his hand was not aimed to kill by James alone, and the guiltiest are amongst us without shame at themselves or respect for others every minute, hour, day, world without end, amen. Mrs. Glencross was the concerned citizen who contacted the Work Farm and helped the caretakers track Alma through the cold-snapped flurrying town, trying to guess where mad sorrow runs, until finding her atop Sidney's grave (for which Mrs. Glencross, guided by unspoken guilt and honest anguish, had secretly paid) facedown with snowflakes resting on her back.

At the Work Farm she fell more deeply into the hole, the blue hole that beckons beneath all our feet when lost for direction or motive for moving at all, the comforting plummet past common concerns and sensate days, down the blue gaping to the easy blue chair that becomes ruinous for its comforts provided in that retreated space, and it takes from years to forever to garner enough replenished zip for the stalled occupant to merely stand from the soft blue avoidance, let alone walk back to the hole and climb toward those known perils of the sunlit world.

For two years she sat facing a yellowish wall in a room without decoration. The room held another woman who stared at the opposite wall and they sat that way without speaking to each other but speaking often, ate when spoon-fed and slept sitting in their chairs. In 1935 Alma developed pneumonia and the doctor gave up but her body didn't. The Work Farm cook, Miss Daiches, who'd been in service for many years to the Etchieson family on Grace Avenue, and had during that time often relaxed for a spell amongst maids gathered at the Greek's, began to pull Alma to her feet daily and make her walk and spit heavily into the hallway spittoons. Kate Daiches walked her down the hall and back, and down and back, and after weeks walked her down the stairs and back, and by the next spring she'd walk her outdoors around the two-acre garden maintained by the less damaged residents. Alma spoke in streaks but not sensibly until on a garden walk in June, with dew dampening her feet she stopped and pointed at a wooden stake standing with a vine fallen over slipped string loops and draped limply to ground, and said, "Them 'maters want tyin' up."

Within three months of that utterance she was helping Kate Daiches in the kitchen. The residents admired her fairy-tale hair but not in their soup, so Alma began the ritual daybreak brushing and brushing and pinning she would repeat daily for the rest of her life. She did at first help only with those aspects of cooking that did not require the use of a sharp knife—boiled water, washed produce, tore lettuce, pulled the strings from string beans, measured molasses, sugar or meal, mixed and rolled biscuit dough, washed dishes and put eating utensils on the table. She worked grief out through her fingertips and before the next summer began to hum as she worked.

It was Kate Daiches who told Alma in the kitchen as they shelled peas that autopsy X-rays revealed Freddy

Poltz, when found blown into the alley, had two bullet wounds behind his left ear. Mr Etchieson, the inquiry cochairman, used to gab plenty during cocktail hour at his home amongst friends and he even had the X-rays in his desk and shared them with esteemed guests who questioned his assertion. Half the country club crowd had seen the proof of murder and remained mum in public. Eventually she'd snuck a look at the stark images and saw that the slugs had been closely spaced and remained obvious and lodged inside Freddy's skull. Kate had always wished she'd tracked Mae after she'd been so meanly chased out of town and shared this fact, but hadn't. She did at night search her soul through self-recriminations stated sharply while staring into a mirror, then on the holiest of days raised her chin and asked Mr. Etchieson about Freddy's murder and had been rebuffed and soon after informed that her services were no longer required. But she thought Alma should know and the town should know and wished she had the courage to spill the beans herself, and she did not, but knew who did when well.

"And you are getting well."

After being returned to town by July Teague, one of the first things Alma shared with her new employer was an account of the bullet holes. July already knew of their existence and she and John Teague had been shown the X-rays at a frolicsome summer party on a gin-soaked night that turned both somber and charged with suspicions as they stared and calculated the significance of two bullets behind the ear. Alma and July told each other all they had to tell, or most of it, anyhow, and soon Alma became aware that she'd been hired as an ally in the pursuit of answers as much as she had been for domestic chores. The women got along well on the instant, and Alma settled into a life that though familiar in many details felt fresh on her skin, then went looking for John Paul.

She had been told by John Paul and others that he lived now with the Rooshian, so she asked the exact whereabouts and went there. The old man and the boy and the old woman were at work in the great garden. Alma laid a hand on the top strand of the barbed-wire fence near where they crouched and told John Paul what was most on her mind. "I don't care ever to hear any more talk that you take money from the hand of that man Glencross."

"I caddy for him. At the country club. You get paid for that."

"Caddy for somebody else, can't you? There's other rich men golf."

"Arthur pays me double what the other cheapskates pay, and tips big fat tips, too."

"He's Arthur to you now, is he? Pshaw! I'm still tellin' you to keep away from his company from now on, for good."

"No."

"For good."

"No."

"You're my son, and I'm tellin' you."

"Can't you see I've got work to do? Mr. C and me and Masha need to weed all these rows and get it done before dark."

"I'm tellin'—"

"Tell me 'til you're blue in the face, Mom. I don't much care."

They stayed that way and would until after the war, John Paul not comforted by his mother's presence, her known obsessions and rages had kept him in such wringing turmoil, and Alma said too often how sorrowful she was that her youngest boy had any truck at all with the man who done for his own aunt Ruby, who loved him so, and all those others who died innocent, too. There were meetings of mother and son and occasional meals, but no ease could be found between them. On every Christmas Day John Paul received Alma's standard gifts of two pairs of bib overalls and a can of tooth powder to see him through the upcoming year. He might not speak to her for weeks at a time and that distance came to be accepted with relief by both.

John Paul loved the Cherenkos—Mr. C was the only father figure he ever lived with or learned from and Masha an encouraging presence, long on understanding and seldom cross—and the love was returned. They survived on meager cash and always would but knew how to fend well, and John Paul gave them most of the money he earned. They never asked for money, and if he had none to offer for a week or two or three they didn't bring the subject up or even hint. The evenings were spent with pots of tea, books, and knitting, Mr. C reading literary classics or ancient history in Russian, Masha knitting something warm for the cold days that were already present or soon enough coming. John Paul would on occasion in these quiet moments catch wind of a po' boy raid, melons or cobs or squash being snatched from the garden, and the first time he hopped up to run toward the voices and give chase, but was stopped. Mr. C had raised a weathered and large-knuckled hand and said, "Is okay they take not too much, boy. Let them be away and eat—you are never been hungry?"

After Pearl Harbor was bombed, and as the nation mourned coast to coast and recruitment centers stayed open until midnight to process stampedes of enlistees, both Cherenkos pleaded with him not to rush off to this fresh war and die for some vague and inflamed notions he'd never even examined. Mr. Cherenko had known violence and killing, terror and flight. He'd been a hopeful worker standing in peaceful protest outside the Winter Palace in early January of 1905, and witnessed hundreds of his own slaughtered, shot down in the snow by the army, falling everywhere dead or wounded to be bayoneted by fellow peasants in uniform, but survived that debacle in the blood-dappled snow and saw a few more that went similarly before escaping the country during December of that same year, and now had precious little regard for military actions of any announced purpose no matter how pure or just the rationale sounded to the ear. But John Paul heard no ambiguity in the American bugles and their call to duty, and finally they asked if he'd at least graduate high school first, plenty of chance to then go over somewhere that isn't home and die for Rockefeller, Henry Ford, J. P. Morgan—all wars always about land and gold, boy. All.

"Not this one."

"All."

On Graduation Day, they both took to bed after the ceremony to lie in shadows and darkness and didn't come out, not the first morning or the second, and he made okroshka for them, delivered the bowls bedside without comment, and on the third morning they had breakfast ready when he woke.

There are snapshots of John Paul taken in China, of himself and other swabbies in various seaport dives and cathouses, a local woman with arms draped over him from behind, one sitting on each knee, and empty beer bottles crowd the tabletop upon which he might rest an elbow, sailor's hat askew, an agog grin on his dimpled, pleasured face. In some poses he and the women have misplaced the majority of their clothing, and though in every one of them he'd recovered his skivvies before the image was made, some of the women chose not to don a solitary stitch. In a few he is fully uniformed and dangerous looking, standing on a gangplank, wearing a thick web belt and a forty-five pistol in a black holster, twenty-two or -three years old and off to deliver the military mail onshore in Tsing-tao or other raucous and luring ports. World War II was over, but his service was not, and he was married by then but shipped with all human needs accompanying to the other side of the world, and he stashed his wedding ring inside his ditty bag for safekeeping when going ashore. (I had to protect the photographs when Mom caught me studying them at around age fifteen and tried to rip the entire album from my hands to burn in the yard, and she still searches for it with matches in her pocket whenever she visits and thinks I'm asleep.) On ship at night, seven thousand miles from home, John Paul watched forces of Mao Tse-tung and Chiang Kai-shek blasting artillery at each other in the distant hills, making the night pulse with low crescents of light chased by faded booms. In the months ahead the pulsing crescents came closer, refugees crowded toward the docks in crowds larger than he'd ever seen or would see and more desperate, and eventually he could watch orange tracers flying after sundown, hear small-arms fire crackling amidst heightened pleas from the cornered refugees, and it was time to pull anchor.

In his six years at sea he saw great vistas and the back rooms of irresistible dumps from Nova Scotia to Hong Kong, had his most miserable hours in the Alaskan Sea, got into a fistfight at the Blue Room in New Orleans with members of Les Brown's Band of Renown, and encountered scenes of biblical squalor and horror in Chinese circumstances. He'd strangely never been hurt or truly terrified during the actual war, luck of the draw, though in the postwar years abroad he did on three occasions (Tsing-tao, Tsing-tao, and Halifax) reckon he was about to be stabbed or stomped to death but each time somehow wiggled off the hook and came out okay. If ever John Paul cried once as an adult, it would've been in 1946 when a letter arrived from July Teague telling him that when a savage hailstorm passed at twilight both Cherenkos rushed into the garden to rescue tomatoes before they were pulped by flying ice and caught summer pneumonia, then died at home within hours of each other during the first week of August.

Alma would have been the very first Gold Star Mother in West Table (that distinction went to Mrs. Lee Haas, who lost her only children, Jeremiah and Samuel, in the early months of war when the *Marblehead* was hit, and Mr. Haas, fatigued and disoriented from battering grief, fell asleep on the divan in the parlor still smoking a cigarette and completed their ruin) had the government known the necessary details, but it was not until 1945 that a cable arrived announcing that Seaman First Class James Maurice Dunahew had perished from his injuries on the island of Guam, on or about December 10, 1941. James had gone away with no word of him received (he likely thought a prison sentence awaited him at home and silence would spare Alma from speaking necessary lies to conceal his whereabouts) until word of his death. In the third year after V-J Day John Paul wandered into a San Francisco nightspot near Union Square and met a bartender who'd been a sailor on Guam and a prisoner in Japan and asked if by chance he'd known his brother. "The men called him Asiatic because he'd sailed in those waters and farther over three or four years, maybe five, and liked all those places around there a whole hell of a lot, which not everybody does. Plenty asked the navy to send them somewhere else, but he asked to stay. Asiatic had been in long enough to be plenty salty, you know, and came running down to the beach with only a carbine, like the rest of us had, when maybe five hundred Japs were storming ashore. Some men wanted to lay down on the sand and surrender right off the bat—don't make the Japs angry, since we didn't have much to fight with, anyhow—a few didn't, though, and started shooting, and Asiatic was one of them. The fight...just went pitiful, sailor. No other way to put it. There was a little bunch of marines and a little bunch of us, and...He was alive when they took us, but...you don't want to know."

"I enlisted in forty-two—I can stand to hear whatever is true."

"I'll only say this much, buddy—the Jap officers had swords."

"What'd he do? Tell me."

"Asiatic bucked when they shoved him around," the man said, and made a whooshing sound while drawing a hand across his neck.

If ever John Paul Dunahew cried twice as a man, the second time was that night. He received his discharge papers at Treasure Island and rode those singing wheels on twin rails back to West Table in early summer of 1948, but he never told Alma that her firstborn son had been taken prisoner and beheaded on a faraway beach where the soft air smelled of tropical flowers and coconuts dangled, or that he'd missed the Cherenkos far more than he had her.

Joe Breen didn't fish. Joe didn't hunt. Joe didn't play ball—baseball, football, basketball—he wouldn't even give a try at any game that featured a ball. He didn't do the things people expected an Ozark boy to like doing, and that was noticed, especially by other boys, some of them mean. Joe read his way through the books on the wall at the public library, spent hours drawing pictures on butcher's paper or cardboard, some of them shocking for the shrewd revelations of personality he managed to make manifest in a sketched face. He wandered the rivers and creeks collecting stones, dolomites, quartz, the occasional geode, and shoved them all under the bed in his room where they scarred the hardwood floor, scars yet visible there. When a hog was slaughtered by Dad, he didn't ask to hold the knife or blood bucket, had important home-work to do elsewhere, and when Mom snatched a chicken head off in the yard and tossed it to the cat, he kept his eyes on a blade of grass and waved away floating pin feathers. He could keep his own company and amuse himself for long spells, an unusual specimen of boy sitting under the apple tree alone, ever alone, but quite content keeping company with a rock or butterfly, garden slug or anthill.

Then at the midpoint in senior year a way-tall, sway-necked goof of a brainy girl moved here from Wisconsin and was put into his history class, and Joe Breen had a beginner girlfriend before Friday. Nobody knows how it happened. She must've leaned his way and said something that started them up, because Joe was unlikely to start any conversations with anybody. His mother saw the couple holding hands on the square before she'd heard the girl's name; Molly Steinkuhler. They took to mooning around town everywhere, love-stunned calves that couldn't get enough of licking away on the skins of each other. It could be an uncomfortable romance to watch or hear up close. Very soon most folks accepted as fact that they would marry, though that assumed certainty hadn't actually been mentioned (Joe was eager to attend the Missouri School of Mines and Metallurgy in the fall, while Molly had been accepted into Lindenwood College) by either of the young lovers.

They were both so ill made for the social ramble that folks who cared felt nervous for them when they did go out to join the human parade, afraid one misfit or the other might spill a drink that stained a popular girl's dress, or during a fast song, trip by accident someone given to sneered and eminently repeatable sarcasm, or that mean boys who'd arrived stag would come up with a rough prank and spring it on Joe in front of Molly, make him shrink to nothing in her eyes, and his own. But the misfit couple wanted to do what others do, go out on a beautiful Saturday night and dance in a crowd, and Joe and Molly did, they did dance, danced as long as the music lasted and still are said to be cutting a rug among friends whenever that Black Angel shimmies.

Arthur Glencross wandered the many rooms of his house and felt dead to himself in each. He wept at windows in the more remote chambers when alone at first, and made excuses if caught by Corinne, Ethan, or Virginia, but within weeks stopped offering even halting, incomplete excuses for weeping while standing at windows so strangely, and in the following year on a night of wet black streets and fog that seemed to relay a message for him alone composed in weather, told his expectant and hovering wife: With all the splendid sinning that had gone on between them, it was somehow Ruby in her simplest and most open moments that took his heart and came to mind every hour of every day—those gone-now-forever respites spent spooned together and drowsing in a rented bed, his best parts at rest and touched to her rump, his fingers at her cleaving, the sun dipping to the west sending light through the blinds in bright slats that climbed the walls like a limber staircase. But when the door closed behind they again must not from this time until the next know each other by face or name if they crossed paths or anybody asked.

Corinne said only two large words in response: "I know."

"She smelled good and different in a way that only she did."

"I know what the girl smelled like."

"She knew things."

"I don't doubt that she did."

"She could tease me and have me like it. At the Arlington, one time, the races were rained out because a thunderstorm moved in to settle, and rain was coming down in sheets, rattling the windows, the afternoon gone black, and she became an imp the way she would, curled her hair around a finger, then wanted to dance the Charleston in that room without clothes on, and did, did dance that way, so funny, and . . . she modeled her new hat with a rained-on windowpane for a mirror, naked girl in a hat, standing so brazen at the window to the street seeing herself in the glass, and you know what she said over her shoulder? She said, 'Arthur, it seems like if you really loved me it wouldn't be raining today.'

"I said, 'It's not raining a drop in here.'

" 'Oh? Well, I love you, too.'

"And we . . . we just . . . Ruby made so many hours turn to magic, Corinne, gloriously hot-blooded magic and all kinds of slick . . . and pleasing . . . to touch, and those hours are when I felt altogether alive, the only times, ever . . . ever . . . and they are spun to . . . memories I can't let go of and wouldn't want to, either."

"You can have all those memories, Arthur." Corinne approached in the unlighted room and hugged him from behind, squeezed him at his middle, rested her face against his back. "But please stop weeping where the children can see."

He gave himself to his work at the bank and welcomed the winged loneliness that darted into and out of his chest at any time of the day, in any setting, any company. His drifting at those moments came to be expected of him, one of his oddly winning traits, to disappear briefly in spirit from the table and return abruptly, speaking to the subject at hand. He put in long, long hours and gave himself little rest. Rumors about him and the Arbor Dance Hall had begun before the mass funeral and have never quite faded away and shouldn't. Certain segments of the town found the rumors to be an enhancement, presenting Glencross as a man with some intriguing qualities, being given to wayward romance and possessing volcanic potential. It gradually became known through social contact that he had no burn scarring on his arms at all, but did appear to have a small round divot above his right elbow. Canoe trips, the country club dressing room, swimming pool parties, all venues served to discredit publicly at least one part of his claimed story. He showed no protective modesty on those half-clothed occasions, left his unburned skin on view to be noted and discussed by peers later over drinks.

Corinne said, "Do you want everyone in town to know?"

"That wouldn't be prudent, would it?"

"Darling, put something on and ease my mind."

"It's too late for all that to matter."

In 1932 he would spontaneously launch into a mumbled confession to the other three golfers from his Saturday foursome while standing in the club parking lot. He said it all in an unbroken streaming with his head lowered and gave himself no quarter. He spilled what he knew and shaved nary a detail from his own role. His audience stood between parked cars to listen—Judge MacDonald Swann, J. William Etchieson, and Harlan Hudkins. The men did not react as though they were hearing shocking or even unsuspected news, exactly. The Judge heard him out and said, "To allow a banker to be charged with anything at all in the climate of this Depression, Arthur, concerning that subject in particular, with hatred of bankers running so high generally, might very well result in no trial at all and an impromptu hanging. We need you where you are, Arthur, to protect our solvency. The town needs you to do that. The gone are gone."

He walked daily from home to work to home. If others on his route wanted to speak, he paused and spoke pleasantly enough, otherwise he nodded to men when passing and touched his hand to the crown of his hat and mimed a doffing to women, and continued on his way. His hair turned a stately white and he came to appear rather impressive, well dressed and closely contained. The heartbreak evident in his face attracted women, quite a few, but he craved only one in the grave and loved one at home and that was enough, so he doffed when approached and flirted with, but kept walking. On arriving home he would every evening go directly to the study and pour a large scotch whisky into crystal and sit in the swivel chair at his desk as night came down or evening stretched.

One day stuck at his window inside the bank, staring absently at sunbeams and movement, he observed John Paul lugging newspapers around the square and those wings took flight between his bones and he stepped out of doors in pursuit. He caught the thirteen-year-old by the arm, startling him. "I want you to consider becoming my caddy."

"I don't play that game—I've never even seen it played."

"You needn't play—I play—you caddy. That's how golf works, Dunahew."

John Paul was on the bags twice a week after that and always overpaid for his efforts, overtipped, and deep down understood why he received such largesse, but the do-re-mi came in so very handy. Glencross knew what he was doing on the links, a fine golfer, tall and limber, long off the tees, good touch around the greens. He became very informal with John Paul, made shrewdly penetrating wise-cracks about his golfing companions, a few of which John Paul employed in self-defense many years later at Hudkins. The two became easy with each other and John Paul enjoyed those outings more than he believed he ought to, but...Eventually the caddy began to whack a few balls along the way, and Glencross watched, then said, "You are innocent of instruction and swing freely. Learn the rules, but don't listen to anybody who tells you to change that swing."

When the Great Depression had begun to lift elsewhere, Citizens' Bank surprisingly developed a rupture, a serious crisis, and Corinne and her worried parents quietly took a huge risk and loaned two hundred thousand dollars of family money, and Glencross sweated bullets day and night but did keep the bank going and once again solvent, and few depositors ever knew of the rupture. Nobody in town lost life savings entrusted to his care. Postwar politicians curried his favor and sought donations and in return he pushed them to open a modest extension of the state university in West Table, which was built and opened to freshmen and sophomores in 1961. Glencross never forgot that he'd had to leave the myriad pleasures of schooling before he was ready because of money, only money, and quickly created a scholarship program for locals of high merit but no financial resources, and eight students a year had their futures buffed and worlds expanded. When apprised of the need, he personally helped recruit doctors to the area, wined and dined and otherwise inveigled enough good docs that he soon pressed for a new hospital to be built, and thus the only sizable medical facility within a sixty-mile radius then and now came about.

At the hospital's groundbreaking ceremony during Au-

gust of 1963, only five months before a cerebral hemor-
rhage claimed him (his body fell on the square within a
few paces of the spot on which his statue stands), he said
to a reporter from the *Scroll*, "This town might grow now
beyond even my own dreams for it."

In spring of 1953, John Paul had been broke, between
jobs, without prospects, and his second son was newly
born (born with pneumonia and something else more difficult to diagnose, and Dad was for many years knotted
with deep worry that it would prove to be a repeat of
the nightmare Sidney knew) while he lived miserably at
Hudkins and his marriage frayed. He went for marathon
walks alone to burn off excess energy and accumulating
hostility, walking at high speed with his hands in his pockets and his eyes looking down, and on one such walk a
black Cadillac shadowed him up Jefferson Avenue late on
an inanimate Sunday afternoon, crept alongside, crept and
crept until John Paul turned to face the windshield, his expression sullenly asking the question, What the sam-hell
do you want? Glencross lowered the driver's-side window,
and said, "Dunahew, I've got something for you. Something I've owed you for a long time—I forgot to give
you an adequate tip on a soggy day in 1938, I believe
it was. With accrued interest and substantial penalties I
must absorb because of my thoughtlessness, it comes to
this amount—come over here."

He handed John Paul a wad of greenbacks that appeared
to have been grabbed blindly out of a bag, an unordered

nest of crinkled bills that when straightened were tallied at more than seven hundred dollars.

"I can't take this, Arthur."

"Hogwash."

"It's too much."

"No, no, you earned it—I beg you to let me pay my debts and feel freed of them."

A memory that had come to mind so often and that he mentioned many times to Corinne during dwindling, melancholy hours, was about how close he'd come to being murdered for love, actually murdered for love—that when James Dunahew stabbed him, he recognized how deeply bound together he'd become with this family from a shack, as James wore a shirt he knew, he was being stabbed to death for reasons rooted in love by someone wearing his own old shirt, a shirt he'd given Buster, who he'd failed so, and as the boy sat atop him and the blade went in again, their two breaths were joined as a cloud in the cold air between them and hung there, just hung there, a cloud.

It just started coming. The story poured from her in dollops and cascades and drips of known details, vintage innuendo and flat-out guesses. She gave her summation of the tragedy while lying in bed, sick at the stomach (too many ears of sweet corn), with pillows stacked behind to prop her at a reclined angle, long hair unbraided and released to drape onto the hardwood floor with the surplus spread there as pooling below a waterfall. She told me to fetch a glass of water and mix in a teaspoon of baking soda. The sun was still up but diving so that stripes of light glamorized the ceiling and made a loamy glowing there. It was Friday and I'd be going home on Sunday and she had more to tell, more for me to know, more to remember. She drank the water, waited for a good burp to erupt and be relished, beat the pillows into shape, sat a little taller and tied it all together for me.

On this, the day of her death, Ruby DeGeer came to recognize her true feelings and feel compromised by the truth they revealed—she still loved the bigwig sonofabitch, she must, since forgiveness is one of the signs, right? Forgiveness felt so icky, slimed at its core, but she'd achieved some perspective without intending to do so and unhappily conceded that there hadn't truly been much point in Arthur courting utter ruin, though what he did that day Buster died and how would always stink of base treachery and mar him in her mind, but... she woke that Saturday at the farmhouse of Captain Reg Gower, late of the U.S. Army, who'd resigned his commission at Fort Dix upon the death of his widower father and come home to tend the family spread of seven hundred acres out along Lost Spaniard Creek. She made him breakfast, one arm in a cast, one whipping eggs in a skillet, and as he ate she saw Arthur with his sleepy way of looking at her from a soiled bed, that tip of tongue, and wished so that he was the man now swallowing her biscuits. The thought made her feel weak, weak, weak without honor, yes, and though this weakness might well be a treason sprung by her heart, it felt too honest as love to argue with much. She'd never had feelings strong enough to override momentary whims or avarice before, or known a man she wasn't willing to drop from her life casually or cruelly at a moment of her own choosing and laugh or sing as she sallied away.

Captain Gower said, "One heck of a spread you set, kiddo—great biscuits. Your mama sure showed you how to do."

The house was large, plain and tidy, with big windows to let in light, and the bottomland just below was dark and excellent growing dirt, with plenty of decent pasture up the slope and around the ridge.

"My mother didn't have a nose."

"She what?"

"Only half a nose—more coffee?"

"How'd that happen?"

"Just living. Something you don't see got her."

"Maybe one more cup."

Alma was fond of many country sayings and she said a favorite here: "A wolf will always look to the woods, no matter what you feed it."

Freddy Poltz stood in the garage under the Arbor, washing automobile parts in a bucket of gasoline, rubbing them dry with rags he tossed when sopped into an old washtub in the corner. He worked alone on Saturdays, and three vehicles were parked in the bay for him to diagnose and repair and slap back together. The old and wide dairy barn doors were open and the day was sunny and he saw two long shadows growing tighter on the floor as they drew near. Two men wearing brim hats and sagged expressions. The smaller man said, "Did you kill my brother?"

"Is he dead?"

"He ain't been home for supper in seven months."

"That's not the same thing as bein' dead."

(Sheriff Adderly testified at the first and only Citizens'

Commission Inquiry that he'd been visited on that morning by a St. Louis–acting man, if you catch my drift, who asked about the unidentified body that had been found at Saunders Camp the previous November. Shot located the only evidence, a hat, in the storage closet, and handed it over for inspection. There was bloodied muck dried at the crown and on the brim. The man slowly looked inside, read the label, raised the hat to his nose and inhaled several times without speaking. He held the hat at his face with his eyes closed quite a while before handing it back. He stood from his chair and said, "No, that ain't Mikey's.")

"It probably is."

"Why are you askin' me, anyhow?"

"I got myself locked up in the county until four days back, Plug, or I woulda been in the boondocks here askin' you sooner, when your memory mighta been better. This here, see, is the last place anybody knows Mikey was, and he mentioned to another guy who ain't personally dead yet that he seen you here in this piss-hole, big as life."

"What do you want?"

"That bank up there. I went broke sittin' in the can, Plug—you know how that song goes. So we're here on a scout and plan on bustin' that thing open tomorrow night. We came here with enough juice to blow that box—they got a thick one—and maybe four more joints this trip round the sticks, and we're parkin' our car out of sight in here so nobody starts wonderin' about it."

"There's a dance upstairs tonight."

"I didn't ask to park upstairs."

"The place'll be jam-packed and jumpin'."

"Clear us a goddam space, Plug. And play nice—you got a wife called Mae and two midgets, don't you? I heard you did."

Alma put another country saying here: "Times there ain't nothin' for it, but a body must hie to the toothache tree and scrape hisself a cure."

There was on that day a garden luncheon down Curry Street at the home of Judge Swann. Tables were arranged on the grass beneath the shade trees, with festive table-cloths and complete place settings and a menu of cold potato soup, spring lamb with mint jelly, early greens, pickled corn, creamed English peas and black walnut pie. Alma and Kate Daiches were present as wait staff and kept the courses coming. At the rear of the yard (a yard two witnesses would that night later spot Arthur Glencross running across with a panicked look) a small stage of rough planks and two-by-fours had been hammered together, with canvas spread on the flooring and a bed-sheet suspended as a curtain on a rope tied between two bent trees. Once the dessert was served, the younger children of those couples assembled there—Swann, Glencross, Etchieson, Haas, Barry, Josselin, Powell, Dacre, Heenan—appeared from behind the curtain to unleash a backyard theatrical, a common feature at gatherings of these families.

Glencross groaned at his table, not in the mood, wearing white linen, not eating, obviously out of sorts. The sight of his own children performing failed to buoy him and he was impatient for the show now started to come to an end. The theatrical was a patched-together mélange of novelty songs presented by a coed group of elementary school hoboes sitting around a campfire made of crumpled red wrapping paper. They had blacking on their cheeks and chins to suggest whiskers and dressed in raffish rags and sashes and held sticks onto which plumped kerchiefs were tied. It was expected that the children would guilelessly deliver songs that were sassy or saucy and containing multiple meanings they didn't suspect and sang of with unknowing purity, and these sly ditties always earned the largest eruptions of laughter and subsequent applause. The hoboes opened the show with "The Men Will Wear Kimonos By and By."

Glencross excused himself to go indoors, where he found the den unoccupied and helped himself to a tumbler of the Judge's bourbon whisky, not his preferred libation—too sweet—but he drank it down in one long movement. He was pouring another of equal measure when he saw Alma pass in the hallway. He called her to him: "Where is she?"

"Couldn't say."

"You've got to tell me. Tell me now."

"I imagine she's with her new fella."

"Does she already love him, you think?"

"I'd say so—they spent two days last week layin' out

there in the country thinkin' up baby names. He likes Lloyd or Mabel, but she..."

He rushed through the hall, out the front door and onto the sidewalk, found his Phaeton at the curb, and drove furiously away toward Lost Spaniard Creek. Several people who knew him saw Glencross speed past without so much as looking to the sides in traffic or pausing at crossroads, just held his eyes straight ahead and kept speeding. Three miles short of the Gower spread, Glencross ran over a farm dog that gave chase, the impact and squealing shaking him alert as he clipped a fence pole and found the ditch where two tires burst. He staggered out from behind the wheel and leaned against the rear fender. The dog wasn't dead yet. The dog he'd run over had mashed hindquarters and wasn't dead yet or quieted, and Glencross began to weep, sob, shudder. The nearest farmer came from his house still energetically chewing something, with a shotgun in hand, approached the dog, did the loud and merciful thing, then negotiated a fat fee of seven dollars to drive this dapper crybaby—it's only a dog, mister—back to town and leave him off near the bank.

About then the Dunahew boys were in the yard outside their shack, James experimentally smoking a green stogie-stub he'd found in the gutter, Sidney and John Paul envisioning the trees as castles and climbing high onto the parapets to claim this palace and all its lands for the one and true king, whoever he was. The bark had been worn from the limbs by scrambling kids at play, skinned to whitened lengths that shined and were slick to climb across, adding more danger to the amusement—kids fell, kids sniffled, kids moaned on the dirt, then stood, shook their heads, and climbed whichever tree again.

Alma returned from the luncheon carrying treats for her boys, and they feasted on wedges of black walnut pie presented to them with only a bite or two already gone, and shared a large bowl of creamed English peas. Tummies pretty full, grins alive, all was well. When Ruby dropped by later that afternoon, the women went indoors to talk and stood beside the tilted sink. Ruby said to her sister what she felt she must, she had to be honest though she knew there'd be hurt piggybacking on this honesty, but what she felt was real, sister, real, and rose up from deeper inside than she ever knew she went, and she spoke her heart aloud.

Alma responded, "No, you won't, either."

"But it's what I feel."

"If you do, you best start lookin' for a new sister, 'cause you won't have one here no more."

"You don't mean that."

"Do I seem like I don't?"

Toward dusk the crowd began to gather at the Arbor Dance Hall, as couples and foursomes and lonesome hopefuls walked down from the Stockman's Café or the Two-Way on the square, drove in from the countryside or strolled over from homes nearby. The street was soon lined with cars parked faced in both directions, and new arrivals pulled onto the grass across the street. The manager of the Alhambra Hotel was firm that no cars could park blocking his entrance or in his small lot and stood on the veranda, arms crossed, watching. Preacher Willard, with his flock in tow, sat on a fence rail down the street and waited for his usual audience of blasphemers and swaggering pagans and trollops with painted faces to assemble in sufficient number.

Arthur Glencross snuck along early with a wavering roll to his steps, and on the advice of the booze within entered Freddy's garage and found himself a hiding spot. He needed to sit and soon but not where he could be seen. There was an interior stairway to the dance hall and the door upstairs was kept locked from this side, but he sat on the top step in perfect shadow and listened as folks entered and shuffled their feet on the squeaky floor and the band warmed up their instruments. He soon fell asleep with his head thrown backwards against the locked door and his legs stretched two steps down.

He woke in darkness to the sounds of jumped-up music, the flying feet, the bubbly roar of communal fun. The carefree music accompanying belonged to those who could be happy on this night, and he was not among that crowd—no way to be happy, maybe never would be again, as heartbreak can take hold and last far longer than mere scars and he sensed that to be true without quite knowing it from experience yet. He listened with his ear to the door for her voice, didn't hear it, her laughter, no,

someone shouting her name, huh-uh, pondered the pleasing possibility that she might not have attended the dance
after all, but decided to ... then, there it was in the sudden ebb of sound between songs, her voice, her voice and
her smell, he was certain he smelled her as well as heard
her say, "Oh, no, I don't, Captain, but it's pretty decent
of you to say so." He pulled the Teacher's bottle from a
stretched and misshapen coat pocket, raised the rump and
chugged some cure for what presently ailed him and might
lame him now and forever, and ... he must put a stop to
this humiliation of his own making, these discordant feelings squabbling inside his chest while his thoughts turned
now to meanly belittling himself for those damned effem-
inate responses—the schoolgirl weeping, sobs in front of
a dirt farmer, for God's sake, while the generalized joy upstairs was insufferable, and demeaning to his person that
so much pleasure came to so many nincompoops on this
night when he would know none at all, and he was the
one who counted, goddam ... If they smelled smoke the
pleasure would stop, the music would stop, they'd abandon
the dance floor and chase down the outside steps coughing
into the street, where Preacher Willard would blister them
with his Old Testament tongue, and they might maybe
blame the preacher, too. He could pull a prank like that,
and when the smoke was more or less cleared they'd return
upstairs but it wouldn't be the same, not after a sudden
dose of fear had run in their veins and trembled their
hearts.

He needed rags. Or straw. Rags or straw or a piece of tire and some newspaper pages. He stepped down into nearly complete darkness, only one small light shined above the opened doors, and began to feel around on the garage floor, walked over the stains from leaks and spills, into the corners, and found a scrap of cardboard, a grocery sack wadded, and a washtub with rags inside. He built his fire on the second step from the top, sack underneath, cardboard on sack, then rags to make ugly black air that would be sucked through the gap at the bottom of the door and stream plumes of black stink in among all the twirling Jacks-and-Jills with their puny joy, and he held a match to the sack, hustled toward the outside door. He turned to watch the fire make black smoke, and it might've made some, he couldn't tell, but those rags popped with flames in only seconds.

He decided to get away and aimed for the door again, but of a sudden felt awful, small, silly and small and awful, and turned around to go kick out the flames he'd made but didn't want now. He stumbled on the first stair, wobbled backwards reaching for anything to hold him upright and heard three men snapping at each other in the alley just outside the door—"No, you won't, either."

"I can't have you parking that juice in here, so—"

"For chrissake, grab him, you Irish donkey." Then the same voice said several words so snarled and low their specifics were lost, but the tenor of the snarling was easily understood, and Glencross began again to fall and reached out, knocking something made of thin metal to the floor at the same moment that two gunshots were fired near the door, their reports lost in the music to those upstairs, maybe, but not in the garage, and the men with guns heard the metal clank and spin on concrete, saw a silhouette of Glencross, and shot. It felt like a shove, a hard nudge in the arm, but he raised a hand and touched blood and the suddenly burning staircase tapped heat to ground and a thin trickle of blue flames ate grease stains, gas stains, any stains on the floor and moved fast as a bad idea to the vehicles parked inside. He crawled toward escape in white linen, not exactly hidden, bottle cracked in his pocket, whisky running down his legs, past tires that were already holding flames, and stood then, and would always feel certain he was at that instant shot at again, at least once, but he made the door and ran. He looked back and saw them coming while flames behind began to rear up and hiss. He went into the alley—he was seen by folks sitting in the upper windows to catch a cooling breeze, but none who survived understood what they were seeing or who was running— and the gunmen were so near he leapt sideways over fences and scooted on grass across yards, under bushes, but did not feel hidden and ran on in a whitish crouch. He heard the hoodlums searching, but turned onto Curry Street and dove into a backyard. (Judge Swann's, and both Mrs. Swann and her hired girl, Bettina Wenders, saw him from the back porch so clearly that Bettina thought he was calling on the Judge and said, "No, no, he's resting now.") He went over another fence and pushed up Hill Street and the world behind him broke open and flew into the air, and he turned to the sky fired by a risen fount of orange that swayed in a tower much taller than the skyline, and became still, saw a building crumpled to bits flung in the air and people falling, and he was unable to move, unable to move or look away, heard the enormous shrieks, the cries, the roasting in their agony, and would never know a day or a night when he didn't.

About the Author

Daniel Woodrell was born in the Missouri Ozarks, left school and enlisted in the marines the week he turned seventeen, received his bachelor's degree at age twenty-seven, graduated from the Iowa Writers' Workshop, and spent a year on a Michener Fellowship. *The Maid's Version* is his ninth novel. *Winter's Bone,* his eighth novel, was made into a film that won the Sundance Film Festival's Best Picture Prize in 2010 and was nominated for four Academy Awards. Five of his novels were selected as *New York Times* Notable Books of the year. *Tomato Red* won the PEN West Award for the Novel in 1999, and *The Death of Sweet Mister* received the 2011 Clifton Fadiman Medal from the Center for Fiction. *The Outlaw Album* was Woodrell's first collection of stories. He lives in the Ozarks near the Arkansas line with his wife, Katie Estill.

BACK BAY · READERS' PICK

THE MAID'S

VERSION

A Novel
by

Daniel Woodrell

An online version of this Reading Group Guide is available at littlebrown.com.

A Conversation
with Daniel Woodrell

Your latest novel, The Maid's Version, *feels like a palpable "something different" from you, even as it's recognizably a Daniel Woodrell novel. When you first started to work on the book, did you have that in mind—to do something more complex and challenging?*

Well, I'm never going to write *Winter's Bonier* or anything, so I'm open to something different. But the story forced some of this change onto the page. There just wasn't any other way to put it together that felt right to me. The language is my language, but gauged to the wider variety of characters from a wider variety of economic circumstances involved. This book sounds more like me as I am now, and is likely the first move in a direction that will call to me for two or three more.

For as long as I've been reading you, which is a good few years now, critics have been comparing you with Faulkner—and The Maid's Version *feels to me like the most Faulkneresque of your novels. Is he an influence or is the mention of his name one of those things that have you slapping your head with your hand and bemoaning lazy critics?*

Hey, I revere Faulkner. He's sitting on the steeple, but there are a lot of figures sitting there beside him. Any small-town

American setting will bring forth "Sherwood Anderson" or "like Faulkner's postage stamp" and so on. I can't kick about the name coming up, as he is in there pretty deeply, but so are Hemingway and Jack London and Flannery O'Connor, as well as several hundred more who had their impact on me along the way. But if I have to be labeled (and basically the world insists that a writer must be categorized, then sub-categorized) Faulkneresque actually leaves a lot of latitude, because the man tried a lot of things.

The plot of The Maid's Version, *it strikes me, is neither quite linear or quite non-linear. At the beginning of the novel, the narrator tells us of his childhood and his adult life, and the memories drift like smoke between the two poles, much as they do in life when you think back on stuff that has happened. I wondered, when you were crafting the book, did the style of telling determine the material or vice versa?*

I knew what I was feeling, and it was only after banging out a bushel of pages for the wastebasket that I realized I needed a different structure to make this work. I did want it to work, in some part, the way memory works, but also the way oral storytelling works—the good barroom bards often seem to be wandering, interesting wandering, but...then their tale shifts back into focus and you see what connects the tendrils to the stalk.

I do think the way you tell a story is as important as what you tell.

I was going to ask what inspired you to write your first historical novel since Woe to Live On *and then I realized there was a historical short story or two in* The Outlaw Album *(and actually "The Horse in Our History" reminds me a lot of* The Maid's Version*)—and then I got to thinking about the recently reissued* Bayou Trilogy *(in which Rene Shade, for example, is frequently given to musing on his past—his relationship with his brother and his father, his relationship with Shuggie), and it struck me that you have quite a complicated relationship with history. Would you say that the implications of the past on the present were one of your recurring themes?*

Like anyone, I'm always reinvestigating the past. I expect that will become more central rather than less from here on.

And, "Horse" was written several years ago, but it was indeed an attempt to tell a story in a way that became useful when writing this—I wasn't sure I'd ever write *The Maid's Version* at the time, but I was turned on by the method of blending yesterday and today through structure. I had been reading a book of nonfiction by Jack Finney called *Forgotten News,* and I stayed up 'til dawn, then wondered how he'd told the tale of an actual event in New York during the 1850s and so completely swept me away. And it's much harder to sweep me away by now, but he did. He told history with a human voice, even an occasional intrusion upon the narrative, and it worked.

I reread the three books that compose The Bayou Trilogy *before speaking to you (I don't have the trilogy, I have three differently sized paperbacks with stiff spines and yellowing pages). Can I ask how the reissue came about? Although the books are related, were they always* The Bayou Trilogy *in your mind or was that a device that was created to repackage and reissue?*

I did not expect those books to be published again. The last came out in 1992, and it seemed they'd remain lost in the deep. I'd gone as far as I wanted to go with them, though I was offered encouragement to write a few more. So, no, I never thought of them as a trilogy, but when the notion of republishing them came up, I recalled the many times I'd bought reissues in trio packages (Elmore Leonard, Daniel Fuchs, Simenon, Chandler, Durrenmatt, Shelby Foote's novels), and my editor liked the idea.

I first came to your writing through The Death of Sweet Mister, *with the Dennis Lehane and George Pelecanos quotes piquing my interest. It was one of those novels you get from time to time (although nowhere near frequently enough) that blow you away and have you forcing them on strangers in the street. When I went back and caught up on you, I wondered how* The Death of Sweet Mister *fits in your life. It feels to me like a book written by an author who has just realized he can do this for a living, a writer who has finally relaxed into his vocation. Was that the case?*

Well, I did this for a living even before it was actually a living. I have survived as a full-tilt freelance writer and nothing else since the early 1980s (for many years my idea of "a living" did not rise to that description in the eyes of most folks I knew). But with *Tomato Red,* then *Sweet Mister,* I felt I had turned some sort of corner. The pure tragedy of *Sweet Mister* resonated with me, and I don't think *Winter's Bone* would've happened had I not written *Sweet Mister* first. One piece of writing paves the way to another, even if the first piece didn't get published, went into the trash bucket—it still taught you what you needed to know to later create some other book, or notable portion of one.

After The Death of Sweet Mister *came* Winter's Bone. *Did the success of* Winter's Bone *change things for you? Did that success make* The Maid's Version *possible?*

I've never had an actual hit book, so no, I don't think my attitude has changed much. *Winter's Bone* did better than the others, but none of the others did anything much when originally published. Life sometimes instructs—after *Winter's Bone* life events occurred, and I realized that I needed to go down a fresh road (fresh to me, at least), and I still feel that I am in that cycle. Looking over the ten books, I can see that about every third or fourth it's time to move, chase down some other path. Change is mandatory, you gotta allow for that, so take a chance, break through, or break down, and start over. If I was on novel eighteen in a series and had to get started on nineteen and make sure it was as much like eighteen as eighteen was seventeen, I'd jump out my fucking window, and since my fucking window is only eight feet above the ground, it would amount to a Sisyphean suicide attempt, I guess, requiring many, many jumps, but if the writing racket doesn't stay jazzy for me, I'll do something else.

I read an interview with Paul Auster a few years back, and he was talking about how he had finally written all of the novels he'd had in his head—and that from here on in, everything he created would be "new" (as it were). That was in my head as I read The Maid's Version. *Has this novel been in your head for a while?*

The Maid's Version has been in my head for decades. There was an event that was similar in many ways, and it happened here—both sides of my family lived hereabouts when it happened. I heard about it from them all. But the way to write and structure the book didn't come to me until I had been writing away for a year. Toss, start over. I don't think I would've been fair or generous in spirit toward all classes involved in the tragedy had I written this twenty years ago, and that approach would've stunk on ice.

But I agree with Mr. Auster—most of what's ahead will quite possibly come from another source.

Cormac McCarthy is another writer you are regularly compared with. Obviously he is now writing directly for the cinema with the screenplay of The Counselor, *which Ridley Scott made into a movie. Have you ever been tempted to write directly for the screen?*

If a director I admired asked me, I might very well give it a go, but I am not otherwise drawn to the bright lights in the mirror.

How important is a sense of place to what you write? How much does the place you live inform what inspires you?

At a time when I was searching, this place, the Ozarks, began to speak strongly to me, and that has been consistently the case for six books now. I've known other places well and may want to use that knowledge, but I'll never feel I've known any other place for generations the way I do here. I plan to be in Wales next April, though, and may well have an epiphany or two while squatting in a Druid circle or puking outside a pub.

Who would you consider your contemporaries to be? Who would you include among your influences?

The living and the dead.

Do you still see yourself as a crime writer—did you ever?

I never did see myself as a crime writer, just a writer. I loved Hammett, Chandler, Cain, McCoy, Thompson, and a passel more, but I knew I wanted to explore on my own and find whatever comes. I always cared more about the characters than crime, or devilishly clever plots—it's all about people. This fetish about labels does grate and limit—Chekhov, "All labels are a form of prejudice."

Raymond Chandler is as stylish and witty and evocative as anybody would want to be. Jim Thompson conducted wild, crazy experiments in narrative structure because nobody seemed to be looking. I try to pay attention wherever I go, and I've learned as much from that neighborhood as I have from any other.

Last but not least, can you give us a glimpse into what we can expect to see from you next?

It's gonna be about werewolves who attend a fancy prep school that is on a space ship that lands inside a black-and-white television down in our basement when I was seven—my tenderest and most autobiographical novel. Or it could be something else; I never know this far out.

This interview was conducted by Peter Wild and originally published in *Bookmunch*. Reprinted with permission.

QUESTIONS AND TOPICS FOR DISCUSSION

1. The Arbor Dance Hall explosion in *The Maid's Version* was inspired by an actual event in Daniel Woodrell's hometown of West Table, Missouri. Has anything similar ever happened in your neighborhood or town? Or did your family experience a catastrophe many years ago that people continue to talk about? If so, how do the people you know explain, justify, or find closure about it?

2. In an interview, Daniel Woodrell said that it was in the Ozarks that "I learned my values. It's better to be poor than to be beholden. Wealth is not the object of life. Be polite as long as possible and, when you can't be polite, don't run." How do these guidelines inform some of the decisions that Alma, Ruby, and Alek make?

3. Alma Dunahew regrets that "she fed another man's children before she fed her own." The class differences in West Table are clear, yet the residents of all levels are bound together by shared experience—capable of generosity and forgiveness. Were you surprised that

Alek's father, John Paul, chose to protect Arthur Glencross's reputation in defiance of his own mother? Why or why not?

4. There are dozens of minor characters in *The Maid's Version,* briefly but memorably described. Who are some of your favorites? Miss Dimple Powell, a fifteen-year-old victim of the blast; Freddy Poltz, the former gangster from St. Louis; Lucille, the dance hall's substitute pianist; preacher and suspect Isaiah Willard; the "Rooshian" gardener, Mr. Cherenko, and his wife; bookish Joe Breen and his girlfriend, Molly?

5. The novel's structure moves among different points of view and time frames—from Alek's occasional narration and sixties childhood, to Alma and her family's migration from country to town in 1890, to Alek's conversation with his father in 1989. This is the way oral storytelling and memory often play out. Did this natural approach enhance your enjoyment of the book?

6. The trains that pass through West Table are described as "beating past toward the fabled beyond" (page 128). Joe and Molly, young lovers who died in the dance hall fire, "are said to be cutting a rug among friends whenever that Black Angel shimmies" (page 143).

One reviewer, William Giraldi, noted that Woodrell moves beyond strict realism and acceptance to longing and myth. "In its fealty to the Athenian conception of tragedy—that collision of the accidental and or-dained—*The Maid's Version* is one more resplendent trophy on the shelf of an American master." Discuss your responses to this assessment. Did you notice oth-erworldly elements in Woodrell's storytelling?

7. Daniel Woodrell has said that Mark Twain was an early influence on his writing, because his mother steered him toward *Tom Sawyer,* which he read every summer as a child. Did you detect and appreciate the humor in *The Maid's Version*? Could Sheriff Shot Adderly, "a country galoot from some hopeless crossroads" (page 46), pass as a Twain character from another era?